ATTIC T___

EDITED BY JEREMY C. SHIPP

Evil Jester Press

NEW YORK

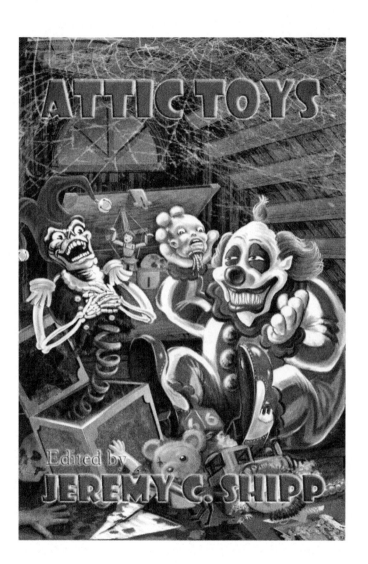

ATTIC TOYS

Edited by

JEREMY C. SHIPP

JEREMY C. SHIPP is the Bram Stoker Award-nominated author of *Cursed*, *Vacation*, and *Attic Clowns*. His shorter tales have appeared or are forthcoming in over 60 publications, the likes of *Cemetery Dance*, *ChiZine*, *Apex Magazine*, *Withersin*, and *Shroud Magazine*. Jeremy enjoys living in Southern California in a moderately haunted Victorian farmhouse called Rose Cottage. He lives there with his wife, Lisa, a couple of pygmy tigers, and a legion of yard gnomes. The gnomes like him. The clowns living in his attic—not so much. His online home is jeremycshipp.com and his twitter handle is @JeremyCShipp.

TABLE OF CONTENTS

INSIDE THE BOXES

Jeff Strand

Yeah, I flunked out of college. I'm not proud of this. Especially because the community college I attended had a pretty low bar for excellence in academic achievement. To flunk out, you either had to party yourself into mental oblivion, or just never bother to actually go to class. I wish I'd gone to class.

Because of this, Christmas was going to suck, suck, suck. I didn't come from a strict household—my parents were very much of the "as long as you did your best" mindset—but they knew perfectly well that if you flunked out of Loribar College you did not do your best. So instead of staying with them in my old room over the holiday, I told my mom that I felt guilty about not spending enough time with Grandma over the years and wanted to stay with her. My mom thought this was absolutely precious.

After I dumped my stuff off in the guest bedroom, which always smelled like vegetable soup for no discernable reason, Grandma and I sat in the living room, sipping hot chocolate.

"You used to love spending your summers here," she said. "Do you remember falling off the horse?"

"I fell off a horse?"

"You were six. It was your cousin Joey's birthday party. We had clowns and a pony. One of the clowns showed up drunk, and your Uncle Rex punched him in the solar plexus. Do you remember that?"

I shook my head. "That seems like something I might remember."

"Well, you were very young. You wanted to ride the pony *so* badly, and we put you on it and you just giggled and giggled and giggled. Then Uncle Rex punched the clown and it startled the pony and you fell off."

"Was I hurt?"

"Oh, no. There was a lot of sawdust around. You were fine."

I laughed and took another sip of my hot chocolate. It had marshmallows in it. Grandma knew how to make some seriously awesome hot chocolate.

"Do you remember swimming in the creek?"

"Vaguely."

"It was a very narrow and shallow creek. It's all dried up now. You used to go fishing in it, even though there was nothing to catch, and one day we came out to check on you and you had taken off all your clothes and were trying to swim in it. You were all scraped up from the rocks. Oh, your grandfather was so mad at you, God rest his soul."

I did sort of remember doing something that dumb. "How old was I?"

"Ten or eleven, I think. Ten, because it was the week before Jasmine's wedding."

"I guess I've always been kind of stupid."

"You weren't stupid at all. You were just young. All kids do that kind of thing. Mostly you just played with your toys. I still have a lot of them, up in the attic."

"Seriously? I thought they all got thrown away." I'd had a lot of action figures that, though they'd been removed from the original packaging and aggressively played with, were probably still worth some money.

"When have you ever known your grandmother to throw something away? I still have your mother's first tooth. Finish up your cocoa and we'll take a look. Maybe you'll find something you want to take back to college."

* * * * *

The attic was so filled with stuff that I'm surprised it didn't cause Grandma's house to collapse. There were precariously stacked piles that literally reached the ceiling, and fire hazards everywhere, but Grandma quickly wove through a narrow path and emerged with a box labeled "Brian."

She wiped a layer of dust off the top of the box with her shirtsleeve, then opened the flaps. She looked inside and immediately smiled. "Do you remember Shelly?"

"My turtle?"

She took Shelly the Turtle out of the box. That had been my favorite stuffed animal as a kid, but somehow I'd forgotten all about him! I took the doll from Grandma, not at all self-conscious about the degree of joy I felt at being reunited with my old friend.

"Do you remember the Shelly voice?" Grandma asked.

I nodded and then held up the turtle, bobbing its head as if it were speaking. I spoke very slowly in a low voice. "Hello, Grandma. Brian wants to know if he can have an oatmeal raisin cookie."

Grandma laughed. "That trick never worked back then, but I think it will work now. I'll go buy some after dinner."

"I was kidding."

"I'll still get you the cookie."

"Thanks!"

"Do you remember Walry?"

I frowned. "Nope." But as Grandma took the stuffed walrus doll out of the box, I had to stop myself from clapping my hands in delight. "Oh, wait, yes I do! Walry!"

I took the walrus from her. Walry had always been one of the most popular inhabitants of my imaginary society, because he could use his tusks to open cans. (Though of course the real Walry's tusks were just white felt filled with cotton and thus unsuitable for opening much of anything.)

"This is so cool," I said. "I can't believe I forgot about them."

"What about Zany? Do you remember Zany?"

I strained to remember any stuffed animal that I'd named "Zany" but came up blank. "Was he a worm?"

"No, that was Wormy. This is Zany." Grandma took a small handheld garden rake out of the box, the kind you'd use when planting flowers.

"I named a rake?"

"Sure." Grandma handed me the rake. "You loved Zany. Don't you remember?"

"Not at all."

"When you fell off the pony onto the sawdust? Oh, you were so angry! You grabbed Zany and you started dragging him across the side of the pony, making long red lines." She laughed. "I've never seen a clown get so upset!"

"I sliced up a horse with a rake?"

"Well, of course. You fell off. It needed to be taught a lesson. If you look close, there's probably a bit of horse skin on one of the tines."

I quickly turned the rake around in my hands, looking for pony flesh.

"Oh, you know I'm kidding. We washed Zany and you used him lots of times after that."

"I really killed a horse?" I asked, feeling sick to my stomach.

"No, no, no. You were only six. You couldn't kill a whole horse, even if it was only a pony. You just scraped it up and made it bleed."

"I truly do not remember anything like that."

"What about the squirrel? Do you remember when Grandpa shot the squirrel that kept us up at night, and then he let you finish it off with Zany? Oh, you went to town on that poor rodent! You even made up a little song about it. Let me think how it went." She began to hum.

"You're joking about all of this, right?" I asked.

"Of course not." Grandma gave me a kiss on the cheek. "There's no reason to be distressed. It wasn't a *good* squirrel."

"But any squirrel—"

Grandma held up a finger to shush me. She hummed for a few more seconds and then her face lit up. "*Squirrel, squirrel, squirrel, you don't get more nuts, squirrel, squirrel, squirrel, now I see your guts.*"

"I sang that?"

Grandma nodded. "For weeks afterward. You were the cutest thing."

"That can't be true."

She looked into the box again. "Oh! Oh! I *know* you remember this one!" She took a hangman's noose out of the box. "Goodness, this thing is tangled up just like Christmas lights."

"I don't remember that."

"Aw, that's too bad. You didn't name it—you were twelve, so I guess you were getting too old for that kind of thing by then—but there was that one man. The religious gentleman."

"What did I do to him?"

"You can still see the bloodstains." She handed me the noose and tapped the rope with her index finger. "See? It's faded but you if you look closely..."

"I can't see it."

"When we go back downstairs we'll look at it under the light. It's kind of gloomy up here."

"What did I do?"

"He rang the doorbell right as we'd started dinner. Spaghetti and meatballs. Your uncle went to see who it was, and, oh, he was so infuriated when the gentleman started talking about Jesus! Your uncle and grandfather held him down on the floor, and you put that noose around his neck, and I remember that you kept saying 'I can't make it tighten!' and we all laughed because everybody knows you don't tighten a hangman's noose. We explained it to you, and you grabbed the end of the rope and ran as fast as you could across the living room, and it popped out of your hands! You landed right on your bottom. But you didn't cry. You got back up, grabbed the rope, and ran again, and this time his neck went *snap*. We were so proud."

"Why don't I remember any of this?"

Grandma shrugged. "There may have been some hypnosis involved. That was all your mother's doing."

"This can't be possible," I said. My ears were ringing and I felt dizzy. "I'm not a killer."

"Well, not very often, anyway," said Grandma. "Usually you were a torturer, or you mangled things that were already dead."

"So what else is in there?" I asked. "A hand grenade? A stick of dynamite?"

"Oh, no. If it wasn't hands-on, you were never interested. Just like your father. Explosive weapons are for the weak."

"I feel like I'm going to throw up."

"Do you want Grandma to get you some Pepto Bismol?"

"No, I just...I can't believe...I'm sorry, but this is freaking me out a little bit."

"It shouldn't. They're fun toys."

"Did I have any more?"

"Of course! I've saved your very favorite for last." She reached into the box and took out a smaller box, this one made of metal. "It's the Ten-In-One Box of Fun! You never went anywhere without it. Look, it even has a little handle." It had a plastic handle, like a lunch box.

"What does it do?"

"Almost everything!" She popped out a corkscrew that had been hidden inside the box like a pocketknife blade. "You've got a corkscrew, which is obviously the best tool for poking out somebody's eyes." She snapped out a small blade. "This one is for more delicate design work, like carving messages into somebody's flesh, while this one—" She snapped out a much larger blade. "—is best when you want to cut off somebody's hand. You could never quite get it to cut all the way through arms or legs, but you could slice off hands and feet like nobody's business."

"How many hands did I sever?"

"Lots." She slid out a square hidden panel that was covered with small spikes. "And here you had spikes, for when you wanted to spike somebody. Sometimes you'd smack them in the face with it, sometimes you'd put it on their back and jump on it, and once you put it on the sofa. You were so disappointed when nobody sat on it."

Grandma continued to slide out hidden compartments. "Acetylene torch, for burning skin to a crispy black. Hammer, for breaking through pesky bones. Bone saw, for when you wanted to get at the brain but didn't want to damage it with the hammer. Refillable vial of acid, for disfigurement. Oversized file, for filing away unwanted skin. And, of course, the electric powered staple remover, for removing staples. You so loved to put in and remove staples."

"I'm a monster," I said.

"But a sympathetic one," Grandma assured me.

She handed me the box. For a brief moment it felt somehow *right,* like I was meant to hold it. Then it just felt like a regular metal box, and I set it on the floor.

"I don't feel good," I told her.

Grandma patted me on the shoulder. "Oh, you poor dear. But be honest with your grandmother; doesn't learning about your dark diseased impulses put flunking out of college into perspective?"

"How did you know about that?"

"Silly. Grandmas always know things like that."

I had to admit, as disturbed as I was by all of these horrific revelations, it was kind of nice to have forgotten about my school problems for a while. Why should I worry about my education when I had such ghastly toys in Grandma's attic?

"Thanks, Grandma," I said. "I really appreciate this."

"I'm glad you're staying with me."

"Can I have some more hot chocolate?"

Grandma gave me a hug. "Of course."

DOWN IN THE WOODS TODAY

Emily C. Skaftun

Today is the day.

At dawn we wake from our paralysis, Mr. Wuzzy and I. He pushes himself up off of his face and stretches, wiggling his embroidered nose, then jumps down from the shelf above your desk, Cherie. He lands gracefully, lightly, as though his age is no factor. I shimmy my own self out from under your arm and your pink comforter and slide to the carpet, and together Mr. Wuzzy and I creep out of the house. I stand on his head to reach the doorknobs.

"Goodbye, Cherie," Mr. Wuzzy whispers, when we are far enough away that you won't hear him speaking. "Do not search for us." Do not search for *me* is what he means. And to some degree, I share his view. Despite the honor and privilege it would bring me, I do not really wish it to be you, Cherie. You keep me safe on your soft bed, and you are rarely rough with me, holding me by the ears or snout or tail.

At the clearing we meet other bears, hugging old friends so hard our stuffing shifts in our bellies. There are bears no bigger than your palm, and some who must be bigger than your whole self. They tower over Mr. Wuzzy and me, but they are still soft and sweet. We beat them every time at hide-and-seek.

Some bears look worse for the year past, but I feel svelte and smooth. My fur is soft and clean; none of my seams need to be restitched.

The day is spent this way, in a spirit of joy, for we know that at dawn the paralysis begins again. We run and tumble and exalt in movement. Some bears do nothing but eat and drink. Some are drunk as plush skunks by sundown. Others climb the oak and maple trees, rustling about in the branches like I imagine real bears must do.

An ancient Teddy Talks-a-Lot hobbles through the long grass, his beak-like mouth opening and closing soundlessly. I think he is singing, but he must have been out of batteries for years. He will never be chosen. At the edge of the clearing, as usual, a clique of Caring Bears share a joint. When I pass by them a Hope Bear yells, "Cheer up!" and the others laugh.

Mr. Wuzzy and I are playing ball tag when the creeping sensation crawls up everyone's backs, making the fur of our scruffs stand on end. Humans are watching.

We are pros; every bear drops instantly, simultaneously. The forest is now a silent place, littered with lifeless toys. Light slices through the trees at a long angle. The ball bouncing through the long grass and off into the trees is the only movement.

I sense a juvenile human weaving through the trees toward us, and I know that it is you. Mr. Wuzzy knows it, too; I can see the panic in his plastic eyes from ten feet away.

You could still remain safe. But then you step into the clearing.

It is all any of us can do not to gasp. The excitement that runs through us is electric, almost palpable. You step right over Mr. Wuzzy and his matted old fur. You step over a dozen bears on your way to me, so gentle, so careful not even to kick any of them. In this moment we all love you, but I love you most of all because I know you are mine.

"Mr. Fuzzy," you say, bending over to pick me up, "what are you doing out here?" You scoop me sweetly up into your arms, not even tugging me by a paw, and pluck a leaf from the fur of my face.

For an instant I'm not sure I can do it.

I look into your innocent face, questioning me as though you already believe I could answer. Then I rear my head back and bare my teeth, pointy and sharp and crowded as a shark's. I wait for your shock; need to feel it. Perhaps I am trying in my own way to give you an escape. But you do not drop me.

And then I bite.

My poison acts fast. You drop like we do, like a rag doll onto the forest clearing, still cradling me in your arms like a precious baby.

In the next moment the bears come to life, cheering and pumping their paws in the air. A few bears look disappointed, kicking stones and muttering things like, *I thought it was my year*. But they do not complain.

Only one bear is truly upset. As I step down from your paralyzed body, Mr. Wuzzy approaches me shaking his head. "We should let her go," he says. "She's been kind to us and doesn't deserve this."

"You're just jealous," I say. I run my paw through the fur on my head, smoothing it down. "You're not her Mr. Fuzzy anymore and now you never will be."

He looks like he wants to say more, but we are interrupted by last year's Chosen Bear. Cuddles is an old bear, taller and thinner than Mr. Wuzzy and I, with the lumpy misshapen look of a comfort object. His fur is even more matted and stained than Mr. Wuzzy's, and one of his plastic eyes fell off long ago and was replaced with a gray button. He grabs my paw with his and lifts it into the air like I'm a boxing champion. All the other bears cheer again. In the corner of my eye I see a Joy Bear clapping her paws across her rainbow-embroidered tummy. When she catches my eye I see her wink.

Cuddles turns back to me when the crowd starts to disperse. "Congratulations, Mr. Fuzzy. What a year you'll have. I must have seen the whole world! It will be hard for me to go back to the stillness again." His plastic eye takes on a faraway look as he rambles, but his button eye holds fast to me. He claps me on the back. "Enjoy the rest of the picnic, son. I'll get everything ready."

And so I step away from your body. I have a Joy Bear to find, a Mr. Wuzzy to ignore, and a picnic to enjoy.

It is difficult to lose Mr. Wuzzy, who follows me around jumping up and down like a young human who has to pee. "You don't understand," he says, but I do not listen.

It is easier to find Joy Bear, and when I do at last old Mr. Wuzzy gets the hint and goes, head down, out into the crowd. Joy bear is forward, nuzzling her pink heart nose into my neck even before we sneak away from the clearing. Already I enjoy being the Chosen Bear.

* * * * *

When the black sky starts to lighten, we gather for the ceremony. You are bound hands and feet in the center of the clearing, and when you see us gather around you your eyes grow wide with fear. It seems now you understand: it's lovely down in the woods today, but safer to stay at home.

Cuddles stands beside you, as does Mr. Wuzzy. He strokes your face, staining his fur with your tears. When the crowd's murmuring dies down Cuddles speaks: "Another year of paralysis has passed. Another year begins at dawn. But before it does, we make this offering so that next year we may again gather here."

He turns to you, gesturing with one paw. He has a flair for the dramatic that I'm trying to memorize. Next year it will be I saying these words. "A human has come here, of her own free will. Who will testify to it?"

The crowd erupts as almost every bear raises a paw and shouts his testimony. Cuddles gestures to me. "Mr. Fuzzy, Chosen Bear, is this your human?"

"Yes," I say. Mr. Wuzzy scowls at me.

"And are there any challenges?"

I am surprised when Mr. Wuzzy raises his paw. "I challenge," he says. A gasp ripples outward through the crowd like a wave through water.

Cuddles looks confused. Never have I seen a challenge, even though it's usually the case that more than one bear is linked to the human in question. The honor belongs to the Chosen Bear. "She is your human, too?" asks Cuddles.

"Yes," Mr. Wuzzy says.

The crowd is loud with speculation. *What happens now?* I hear some ask. A female voice says, *Maybe they can share the heart.* But I look into Mr. Wuzzy's eyes. He does not want to share. He wants to set you free. I wonder if you know the depth of his devotion: without a sacrifice none of us will be released from our paralysis next year.

And so I don't wait for a judgment. "I am the Chosen Bear!" I shout. "Her heart belongs to me." There is a moment of silence before the crowd reacts, but when they do it's clear they are on my side. They cheer for me, and I feel powerful. I bare my teeth at Mr. Wuzzy, running my tongue along each thorn-like point. I do it to make him angry, and it does.

Mr. Wuzzy jumps across your squirming body and tackles me, his own needle-teeth snapping in my face. I am on my back in the grass, but I manage to get all four paws under him and push him away, and he falls back. I charge him like a bull, but he is quicker than me. He grabs me and before I really know what he's doing my face is in the dirt. I think he is stepping on my head, twisting and grinding until I feel the stuffing breaking apart inside, feel the dirt working deep into my fur. Over it all I can hear your scream.

Suddenly the pressure is gone, and I stand up. All around me is chaos, bears hitting each other, grabbing and pulling at fur and ears and tails, stabbing at eyes and biting with their sharp, sharp teeth. The crowd has pulled Mr. Wuzzy off of me, and now they surround him, so many people attacking him that they're hurting each other by accident.

I brush the dirt from my face, afraid of how badly my fur's been damaged.

Cuddles breaks free of the melee and jumps onto your tummy, waving his arms in the air. "Quiet!" he yells, with such force that it cannot be ignored. Bears freeze with paws drawn back mid-punch; they freeze with mouths snarling open.

"The sky lightens," he says, softer now, "and so we must proceed."

Looking chastened, bears get back into order, helping each other up and murmuring apologies. A battered-looking Mr. Wuzzy brushes himself off, even as other bears stand around him like guards.

"Chosen Bear," Cuddles says. "As custom dictates, I leave the honor to you. It is up to you to decide if you'll share with the challenger."

I nod humbly to Cuddles, then glare at Mr. Wuzzy. "I will not," I say.

"Then on your word we begin."

I step toward you and you twist away. "No. No. No," you chant through the tears. Standing on your chest I stroke your face with my paw as Mr. Wuzzy did, and when I look at you I understand how he felt. It didn't have to be you, and perhaps I would even have been happier if it were not you. I do not like to see you so sad and afraid.

But it was you.

"Yes, Cherie," I say quietly, only for you. Then, "Yes!" I say louder. The bears strike as one mass, fast as a pack of snakes. Shark-like teeth surround you from all sides, and we devour you quickly. You do not scream for long.

We eat until there is nothing left, crunching through your bones and licking every last drop of blood from our fur and the grass in the clearing. In our frenzy we even eat your clothes and the ropes with which we bound you. Yet your heart is mine alone, and I eat it slowly, savoring the year of freedom it buys me.

The sky is very light when the last bears leave and I worry that they will not make it back to their homes or stores before paralysis sets in. I am in no hurry. I dawdle, deciding where to go, when I hear a soft moaning from just outside the clearing.

Mr. Wuzzy crawls toward me from the woods. I see a new rip along his side seam, and I think his left eye looks loose. "Mr. Wuzzy," I say, "Did I do that to you?"

Mr. Wuzzy laughs. "No, Fuzzy. I don't think you could."

I reach down to help him up, checking the sky in alarm. The sun will peek over a distant ridge any moment now; Mr. Wuzzy should be home by now. Even as I worry about the sun, another thought occurs to me. "Did you get any of the . . . of Cherie?"

He shakes his head. "Couldn't get through the crowd. For some reason they were mad at me." He smiles again, but weakly, and I realize how much I'll miss his sense of humor. Even during paralysis, Mr. Wuzzy was a pal.

I run to the center of the clearing where the grass is matted and trampled. "Maybe there's some blood left!" We may have missed some in the low light, I think. But I see nothing.

"It's okay," he says. "I was asking for it anyway."

"But the paralysis! Next year—"

"It's okay," he says. "Just take me ho—"

The sun has climbed into the sky, and Mr. Wuzzy is inert again, just a toy. He falls limp onto the ground and I run over to squeeze him, shake him. It's no use. I want to cry, but of course I cannot.

It's hard work, but I carry him all the way back home. There are people about, and so I have to stop frequently to act like a toy. It's noon by the time we get to your house, a household in pandemonium. Your humans are frantic looking for signs of you, but they will never find any, Cherie. I looked myself, but not a drop of you remains.

I use the confusion to enter unnoticed. Your door is closed, so I stand on Mr. Wuzzy's lifeless head to reach the knob, then I carry him the rest of the way to the neatly-made bed. It was never rumpled last night. I push him up onto the bed and arrange him just-so against your lacy pillow, just the way you used to place me.

I whisper, "Goodbye, Mr. Wuzzy."

I take one last look around the room before I go, memorizing everything. Like you, I will never return.

DOLLHOUSE
Craig Wallwork

The cottage Darcy's parents bought was set within the peaceful district of the Ryburn Valley. It stood elevated upon Yorkshire moorland where heather, crowberry and cotton grass grew all the year round. The limestone walls were shades of the moon's darker side, and when the sun settled beyond the hills, the cottage appeared more forbidding than in day. Darcy grew accustomed to the snapping of logs and cinder trails on the carpet that came from the open fireplace, and at times the wind could be compared to a hundred tortured voices baying upon every window pane. But fear never exploited Darcy's mind, for as her father contested on many occasions, all things can be explained. The low thundering rumble that tore a hole in the night was not that of a monster pushing its way from one world to the next, but the nightly groans from the heifers keeping warm in the farmer's barn across the fields. The unexpected squeak of a floorboard was not the heels of a ghost, but instead the yawning of wood as it waned under the heat of water pipes. The illusory evil that supposedly cowered in shadows, or became the cold breath of night that followed her from room to room, was only a mischievous current of air. All could be explained. Everything, that is, save for the dollhouse.

It was a perfect replica of the cottage in every detail. Shaped gable ends, stone quoining to front corner elevations and detailed mullion windows with glazing. The front and its roof opened to reveal the same three story, eight room accommodation. Stair railings, banisters and newel posts perfectly matched the deep mahogany like those her hands touched every day. The roll top bath was finished with similar gold fixtures and ornate feet. The only noticeable difference was the absence of furniture in the rooms. But it was beautiful and well crafted, and would have remained hidden in the attic had it not been for the ghost.

The previous evening Darcy had awaked to a large bang. The wind was an ocean rushing up and down the chimney's flue. Its noise would have pulled the most rationale mind to the presence of something unworldly. But Darcy deduced that a door had been left ajar in the cottage and the wind was moving from room to room with little care for those sleeping. She left her bed and felt the pinch of a cold wooden floor against her bare feet. The faint hue of a silver moon cast the landing in a static haze. Shadows huddled for warmth in every corner and the floorboards moaned and grumbled as each was stirred from their slumber by her tread. Darcy passed her parent's bedroom and pressed her ear to the door. The sonorous breathing of her father bled through the wooden panelling. The door was firmly closed, as was the bathroom's. As she passed the attic she felt a cool breeze and turned to find the door was open. Crude steps made from cheap wood ascended to a blanket of darkness beyond the staircase. Darcy approached and peered in with a quizzical, almost brazen air of displeasure. As her hand reached for the latch to close the door, she caught sight of a willowy form moving across the attic. She was not alarmed by this revelation, and assumed a car had passed outside, the light from the headlamp throwing a wayward shadow across the wall. A small light switch assured her steps as she made her way up to the attic.

Cardboard boxes of various sizes lay strewn across the floor, each labeled for every room in the house. Cobwebs hung from the apex and wooden beams like old rags and the smell in the air was like that of wet shoes and mothballs. A small window confirmed her suspicions that the ghost was only a light passing against the wall. She was about to leave when he noticed in the corner of the room a large object covered under a dust sheet. For years her parents had the habit of hiding gifts and birthday presents in lofts, attics and basements. Her ninth birthday was in three weeks. Darcy crept across the floor and lifted the sheet to reveal the dollhouse. That she had not hinted or requested one mattered little, for upon seeing it in that dimly lit room, she was completely happy to know it was hers.

Her clandestine visits became a nightly routine. Darcy would wait until her parents had gone to bed and then she would visit the attic to see the dollhouse. An increasing number of ornamental furniture and fixtures were being added on each visit that matched perfectly those in the cottage. Her parents must have hired a master craftsman to fashion these items before placing them in the rooms every day. From the sleigh bed in her parent's bedroom to the antique Wellington chest in the living room, and Georgian oak antique chest of drawers in the dining room, the world she physically lived within had been shrunk to Liliputian size. By the first week, wallpaper had been added, and by the end of the second, the same taupe Saxony carpet covered the living room. The biggest surprise came three days before her birthday. Darcy arrived in the attic to discover three small figurines had been placed in the dollhouse. Each resembled in the most accurate detail Darcy and her parents. She took them out and marvelled at the complexity and proficiency of each. Her father's figurine had the same Roman nose, designer glasses and widow's peak. Cheekbones were prominent and neck lacking in muscle. Her mother's hair was styled into the same bob that flanked a rounded face. Lips like clam shells and eyes of onyx. Darcy's effigy wore a pretty blue flowery dress, the same she had in her wardrobe and was her favorite of all her clothes. Her auburn hair was tied into a ponytail, much the same way Darcy preferred to wear it. The nose was delicate, its bridge peppered with tiny specks of brown paint. The scar upon her chin that she had gained when she fell from a tree when five years old was etched into the wooden face of her counterpart. The house was complete.

On the eve of her birthday Darcy visited the attic to play with the house for the final time. She undid the latch and pulled back the front façade and roof. Everything was there, from the tiny furniture to the bowl of quince in the kitchen. Darcy found her wooden parents lay in their wooden bed, just like her real parents lay sleeping one floor below. To her surprise, Darcy's figurine was in the attic, knelt before a smaller version of the dollhouse, the most recent addition to the collection. Darcy moved her smaller self out of the way to get a better look. Again, the miniature dollhouse had been crafted with such skill it was almost too perfect. She did not wish to touch it in case it broke. In that moment her eye saw something move in the dollhouse. Using her finger, she gently moved papier-mâché boxes to one side within the attic area, assuming that a spider may be hiding in the balsa eaves. A noise like that of shifting feet presented itself behind her. Darcy turned and for the briefest of moments saw an image of a man. His limbs were extended beyond that of what could be considered normal. He wore no clothes, and while shadows draped him like a veil, Darcy noted deep scars traversing his torso. The fingers of his ribcage pressed against cyanotic skin, and a long, malformed face like that of a gnarled tree trunk remained devoid of emotion. She had enough time to blink twice before the man disappeared. Darcy sprang to her feet and ran to the area the man had occupied. With each step that pulled her toward the shadows, she convinced herself it was a trick of the light. A mix of fatigue and the sickly hue of the bulb. The space where he stood was empty. Darcy reached her hand out to the pool blackness and it found nothing residing there but a coolness that tightened her skin.

Darcy returned to the dollhouse, and as she reached for the small clasp that secured the front of the cottage, she noticed the figurines of her parents were no longer sleeping in their beds. Her father was in the living room, his little wooden effigy lay suspended by a piece of brown twine; one end fixed to the wooden beam fixed to the ceiling, the other end wrapped around his wooden neck. She found her mother's figurine lying in the roll top bath, a trickle of red paint bleeding from her wrists. Both her parent's wooden faces of powder pink and cream were warped by fear.

A dull thud came from the rooms below the attic, and in tandem her heart beat out a similar sound. Darcy got to her feet and ran down the wooden stairs back to the landing. She opened the door to her parent's bedroom and found a feral landscape of bed sheets and nothing more. She called out for her mother, skewering a cry for her father to its end. More stairs. Two at a time. Down she went. The moonlight was split upon the cold slate floor of the kitchen like a gallon of milk. Darcy slipped as she rushed through it and fell on her back. Pain danced up her leg and spine, elbows throbbed. She clambered up and limped to the door that divided the kitchen to the living room and paused to catch her breath. All can be explained, she said like a mantra. All can be explained. The wind was a werewolf trapped in the walls, the moon a phantom consuming the stars. The house creaked and moaned as though the souls of the damned resided under floorboards. The door's handle cooled her sweltering palm. She twisted it slowly and pulled back, releasing a whimper from the hinges. The gap could not have been more than a few inches, but the naked heel of her father's foot suspended in the pastel shades of a lifeless night was enough to force her to not open it any wider.

She assumed it was tears. The tips of her fingers were darker after she wiped her cheek. Darcy felt another large drop upon her face and she looked up. A patch of water collected on the ceiling, its color brownish in tone. Darcy moved back and every drip that hit the kitchen floor resembled a short-lived scarlet coronet. To her knees she fell, shaking, sobbing. The bathroom was directly above her. Flashes of a naked wrist cleaved to reveal open veins flooded her fragile mind. She scampered to the sanctuary of a shadow, wrapped it around her shoulders and wept. It had to be a dream. Darcy convinced herself of this. Her parents would not end their lives like that. They were happy, and they would have never left her alone. The noise from upstairs suggested something, or someone was still in the attic. If it was a dream, she had nothing to fear. If it wasn't, then it was better she was with her parents than in an empty and cold cottage. Alone.

Legs turned weak. Nightgown, drenched with tears. She passed the bathroom without looking in. At the foot of the attic stairs she inhaled deeply, wiped her eyes and took the first step toward the beyond. The world slowed to a crawl. Silence overruled the clamor of what lain among the flotsam of domestic knick-knacks within the attic. Even Darcy's weight held no influence on the steps beneath her feet. It was though the whole house was holding its breath in apprehension. She arrived in the attic to find it as it was. The boxes were unmoved, the cobwebs sloth-like as they hung from corners. Shadows hugged miserably to the walls and floor. And there the dollhouse glowed like a Halloween pumpkin in the dim light, a macabre symbol of her fate. There was no change to her parent's figurines, which remained in their varying exhibition of death. But Darcy drew her attention to the small attic in the dollhouse. There was the small crafted model of herself kneeling before the miniature dollhouse, just as she was knelt before the larger one. On closer inspection she noted a red line that scored the throat of the tiny figure. The winter's breath she grew to believe was only a draft fell upon her neck in that moment, and from the corner of her eye a hand came into view. The tips of each finger were sheltered by gauze, blood seeping through as if the toil of intricacy and detail had worn the skin to the flesh. Scars as thick as leeches chartered the hand, and the rasp of failing lungs stirred her hair. The glimmer of a small whittling knife constricted her pupils, and upon her throat its cooled edge prevented the words she longed to speak.

All can be explained.

All can be explained.

POOR ME AND TED

Kate Jonez

Glory, Glory, Glory. That's about the stupidest name you can give a person like me. But my mom had high hopes like lots of hard-working folks do. They use fancy names like they're magic spells. As if naming a kid could somehow make it better than it really is. I don't go in for that kind of crap. I named my kid John. Simple. John.

"I know that mess is up here somewhere, Ted. I know it is."

I heave one more of the brown boxes down from where they're piled up and drop it on the floor. It's not so heavy this time. This one must be a box of old clothes even though it says 'kitchen' plain as day on the side of the box.

"Seems like you ought to know which box, Ted, long as you've been up here. You ought to go on and tell me." I laugh about that because Ted never tells. He never does.

I drop the box on the floor and dust rises up in a puff. It ought to bother me more than it does with my damn allergies from all the bad air and all, but the dust motes look kinda pretty, like bubbles, the way they float in the light from the dormer window.

"John would have liked how the dust dances around in the light, wouldn't he, Ted? He would've liked that—at least back when he cared about stuff like that, he would have."

I catch the edge of the silver tape and yank it off. Clothes, I was right. Just as I'm about to close the box back up the smell hits me. Like turning a page in a picture book, one minute you're in a dirty old attic, and one minute you fly back in time to when everything in the world was good and smelled like baby lotion and butter cream frosting. I about put my head right in that box.

"Yeah, I know, Ted. It's stupid to cry over spilled milk."

I fight down the burning feeling that's trying to fill up my chest as I tape that box back up extra tight. Maybe that smell will stay in there. Probably not, though. Probably it'll be gone next time I come looking for it, just like everything else.

I pull down another box from where it was wedged on top of the chifferobe that used to be in my bedroom. Back when I had a bedroom and I didn't have to live in one crappy room because that's all I can afford. I nearly topple over with the weight of the box. It lands on the floor with a thud this time. Bingo. I rip it open.

"Come on over here, Ted. I'm going to fix you up real nice, so we can go out. You're going to sparkle just like the Fourth of July."

I unbutton Ted's coat, and as I'm fixing him up just right that feeling like fire starts burning inside my chest again.

"I don't know why you say it's my fault, Ted. Because it's not. I did everything I possibly could for John. Somebody should have helped me. Wasn't like I didn't fucking ask, was it, Ted? I fucking asked people to help John. They didn't listen."

* * * * *

Union Station is beautiful, probably the most beautiful train station in the world. I walk across the shiny floor polished up like it's Cinderella's ballroom and past the leather chairs all done up with brass tacks and look up at the sparkly chandeliers. Union Station is beautiful, but it's only fake beautiful. If I look under those chairs, there'd be wads of old gum. The bathrooms here are just as nasty as the ones at the Greyhound station. Anyone can go into the train station, and everybody knows a place ain't shit if they let everybody in.

I jam a five into the slot of the Metro ticket machine. Five fucking dollars to ride a damn train. That ain't right. Ain't no way that's fair.

"I know, Ted, life ain't fair. Heard that about a million times."

Ted's looking a little ragged. He could use a new jacket. His is getting a little worn out around the middle. But at least he isn't growing out of his clothes. Not like John did. That kid needed something new every week, it seemed like.

I move out onto the platform to wait for the train. People are lining up. The sun glints off their shiny clean hair and polished shoes and the metal decorations on their expensive briefcases or their Gucci bags or whatever the hell kind of bag rich people carry. They all hold their heads that way so their eyes don't see anybody else. Like their thoughts are so important they don't want them to leak out. I hate that shit. Doesn't matter how much your suit or your shoes or your damn haircut cost, you can look somebody in the eye. Say good morning. How are you? It ain't like I'm going to really tell you how I am or anything. I'm not stupid.

"I know they don't care, Ted. You don't have to tell me. I fucking know they don't care."

I don't know when Ted started thinking it was such a good idea to state the obvious. I don't remember him always doing that when John was around. When John was around, Ted was always telling him stories. Stories with morals and happy endings and shit like that. Lot of fucking good that ever did. John wasn't even listening. Especially not after he got himself a new name. How the hell do you shorten a name like John? The letter 'J,' what the hell kind of name is that? That's a stupid name. That's just asking for trouble.

The ground rumbles under my feet. For a second it feels like the whole damn train station is coming down. "Wouldn't that be something, Ted? Wouldn't that be something to see?" But it's just the train pulling in. The slick steel train all shiny and bright like a new can of air-freshener pulls up alongside the platform. Its doors open with a whoosh. I could have felt the cool air-conditioned air if it hadn't been for all those people crowding 'round the doors. They think they're so fucking important. They think every minute of their day is worth a hundred bucks. If I ask them, I know that's what they'll say. That is, if they'll spend a whole minute on me. Fucking people think their time is worth money.

My old boss used to think his time was worth money. He even said that to me when I had to take time off to be with John, or 'J' as he made me call him by then. I knew I needed to be at work. I knew that more than my asshole boss did. He could take off work anytime he wanted and go to a resort in the Caribbean or some such shit like that. Not me. I miss one single day, and I'm fucked.

I hang back and wait for everybody to get on the train. I could go up there and push my way in so I can get a good seat, but Ted wouldn't like that. It's better if he doesn't get jostled around too much anyway. When everybody finally sits down I find a seat by the door. It's all full of newspaper, but at least it doesn't look like a bum pissed on it or anything.

"Save my seat, Ted." I laugh out loud at this because that's what John used to say before he was 'J.' Before they shot him in the head. Before he became the kind of kid who goes by the name of 'J' and ends up in the wrong place at the wrong time. Always happens. Always does. He was just asking for trouble. Well, he got it, didn't he?

"I'll watch him for you," a little kid says. He plops down in the seat next to Ted.

The kid is maybe seven or eight. His clothes fit him exactly, like his mom didn't ever have any trouble keeping him in clothes that fit. That kid shouldn't be on a train by himself. I look around to see if someone looks like his mother. A kid shouldn't be on the train alone. A kid shouldn't be on the train.

"Not my problem, Ted." The kid has a mother to watch out for him. One of those rich mothers who never have to worry about how their kid will turn out. I did my best, and it didn't do one fucking bit of good. Nothing I can do about it now.

"Alright, you watch him," I say to the kid. I put Ted in the kid's lap, and pat his brown furry head. He was a good friend to John. He always was.

I pull my phone out of my pocket as I walk down the aisle and back out the door. It's a cheap phone like you get at the 7/11, but that doesn't matter. It works. It gets the job done.

I step out on the platform and move down a ways as I'm punching in the numbers.

When I punch the last one the train's doors swish closed. I think about that kid in there with Ted. And how Ted's watching over him just like he used to watch over John before he was 'J.' Did that kid's mother ever worry for one minute, one 'hundred-dollar minute' if she'd be able to keep her kid safe? I doubt it. She doesn't have to. Everything is easy for her.

Fire rises up in my chest and burns like it's going to kill me. What if Ted is right and it really is my fault, all the stuff that happened? That thought makes the fire burn even hotter. I don't worry about that pain, though, because—BLAM!

The blast rattles the platform and shakes Union Station. For an instant, about as long as it takes for a bullet to exit a gun barrel, fly through the air, and blast through my boy's skull, all motion is suspended.

And then, all at once, smoke and fire pour from the twisted metal of the train. Bits of metal, shards of glass, chunks of cement rain down on the passenger's shiny clean hair and polished shoes and expensive briefcases or Gucci bags. They scream, all of them, like they have a fire burning inside.

"Glory, glory, glory, Ted. Now they know what it feels like to be me."

A LITTLE CRIMSON STAIN
Joe McKinney

Donnie Ross knew the little girl was dead the instant he saw her picture in the attic of the Wilmington town home.

He gasped and stopped short. His gaze flicked to Cowen and Curtis, but neither man had noticed his reaction. Both were too busy fussing over a dusty porcelain tea set. Slowly, like two heavy wheels reluctant to turn, Donnie's eyes moved back toward the dead girl's picture. With her eyes closed, one hand nested in her lap, she might have been sleeping. But Donnie knew better. In her black, papery dress, her features as wooden and as doll-like with rigor mortis as the doll she was holding, she was most certainly dead. He swallowed hard. The picture disturbed him, even horrified him. And yet he was completely fascinated.

Postmortem photography such as this was common between 1845 and 1925, though this example was almost certainly from around 1905. It was very Edwardian. Her clothes helped to date her, but so too did some basic history. Until 1900, most middle class families dressed and prepared their loved ones for burial at home, an operation customarily performed in the front parlor. But as professional funeral homes opened up, this tradition became a mark of the provincial and the poor. So much so that in 1910 the *Ladies' Home Journal* issued a decree that the front parlor should be forevermore referred to as the living room. Funeral establishments were then free to adopt the more familiar, and less threatening, attribution of funeral parlors.

Donnie, who made his living as an antiques acquisition agent for the auction house of Harris-Sadler, Inc., had once delivered much the same lesson on an episode of *Antiques Roadshow*, and the show's producers loved it. So much so that they'd asked him back four times. But the dead girl's picture meant that he was probably wasting his time here in this dusty attic. Photography used to be expensive, and death was one of the only occasions important enough to justify the expense. That meant they were a middle class commodity. And that, in turn, meant that everything in this attic was likely to be middle class, too. Donnie sighed. Another road trip wasted.

He scanned the rest of the attic, his practiced eye hoping to catch sight of something unusual as he stifled the need to cough. Intense morning sunlight poured in through the large, open window opposite him. White silky curtains billowed on the breeze. The dust clothes covering the furniture fluttered gently. Opening the window was a wasted effort, he thought. Airing the place out had done nothing for the dust. He was going to be miserable with sneezing and sniffling all the way back to Greensboro. He could already feel it coming on.

And then he saw the doll.

Donnie blinked in surprise. It was a "bebe" bisque doll, he could see that through the layers of dust covering it, but it wasn't done in the usual French or German style. The clothes were simpler, more American. French and German dolls had round, cherub-like faces, with enormously round blue eyes that always reminded Donnie of the anime cartoons of Japan. From its clothes to its facial features to the eggshell fragility of its cream-colored cheeks, this doll, perhaps 24 inches high, was something else entirely, something uniquely American.

Dolls weren't Donnie's forte. His specialty was furniture. But he knew the basics, just like he knew the basics of sports memorabilia and landscape paintings and model trains and a hundred other species of attic treasures. Donnie knelt down next to the little figure and examined its fingers and the joints where the arm pieces met. These dolls usually showed signs of wear, nicks and cuts and gouges in the porcelain, and so the value at auction could range from the ultra rare six figure examples to the modestly worn ones that might fetch a few hundred dollars on a lucky day. This one was very clean. It was better than clean, he corrected himself. It was amazing.

"Is that...?" Frank said, gasping.

Donnie glanced up at him. Frank put his hand over his mouth, stifling a giggle. Herb came over to stand by Frank's side. Both men were wide-eyed.

"Oh my God," Herb said. "I can barely breathe."

"I know," Frank said. He took Frank's hand and squeezed.

Donnie shared their excitement. This was exactly what they'd hoped to find when Frank and Herb first contacted him about this house. The woman whose death had created the opportunity for them to search the attic was the daughter of the fin de siècle actress, Marianne Staples, who at one time had lived with the American doll maker, Christian Mueller. They had two daughters together. Mueller's dolls rarely came up for auction. But when they did, they fetched high prices, even when the condition was less than ideal. If this was an authentic Mueller, Donnie figured, it could bring $130,000 at auction, easily.

Donnie removed a fingerprinting brush from his shirt pocket and gently cleaned away some of the dust from the doll's face. Except for a little dark spot just below the left eye, the doll's condition was marvelous.

He worked on the spot with the brush.

It wasn't dust.

"Can you see Mueller's mark?" Frank asked. "It should be just behind the ear, right at the hairline."

"I know," Donnie said, suddenly irritable. The spot wasn't coming off, and he didn't like people hovering over him while he worked on something as delicate as this. But the more he worked on the spot, the more troubling it became.

Then it hit him what the spot was.

He flinched away from it.

"What's wrong?" Frank said.

Donnie didn't answer. He stood up and went to the little dead girl's picture on the sideboard on the opposite side of the room. The doll she was holding, the clothes were different, but that little spot just below the eye, that little dark stain, it was the same.

"Ugh," Frank said, covering his mouth again. "That's ghastly."

"It's the same doll," Donnie said. "Look at the little crimson stain below the eye."

"It's in black and white," Herb said. "How can you tell that's crimson?"

"Look at the cracked veins around the girl's eyes. Those aren't crow's feet. Not at her age. That girl died of consumption. She was probably coughing up blood to the very end."

"Oh," Frank said. He shivered. "Ghastly."

"Yeah," Donnie agreed.

"What do you want to do?" Herb asked.

"I have to take it with me," Donnie said. "I know an expert in Raleigh. I can stop there on my way home to Greensboro. I'll let you know what I find out."

"Definitely," Herb said. He squeezed Frank's hand again, his grin a mile wide. "This could be a major score."

* * * * *

Before leaving Wilmington, Donnie stopped off at a small diner for an early lunch. He'd taken quite a few pictures of the doll with his iPhone, and after ordering a Diet Coke and a hamburger, he emailed them to Marty Wright, a doll expert he sometimes worked with, and waited to see how long it would take her to call him back.

The waitress didn't even have time to bring him his drink.

"Please tell you have that with you?" Marty said. "You didn't let the dynamic duo take it, did you?"

"Relax. I have it in the car. You saw the maker's mark, right?"

"Oh, I saw it. I can't believe the condition. It was like it was never played with."

Donnie smiled. She was on the hook alright, and it was in deep. "So, you don't mind if I come see you today?" he said.

"Stop teasing me. Just get here."

"It'll take me about two and a half hours."

"I'll be waiting."

He heard the purr in her voice and he felt a sort of hunger stirring inside him. At 36, Marty Wright was among the best in the business. Auction houses and museums from all over the world paid handsomely for her services. He'd once seen her take a representative from Lloyds $143,000 above his initial valuation on a Victorian era closed-mouth bisque head doll, despite the mountain of documentation and research he'd brought with him. She was confident, unrelenting in negotiations, and very beautiful. She was single, too. Donnie's wife hated her.

Still smiling, he hung up.

After lunch, he called his wife.

"Are you coming home to me?" she said.

"I'm headed back that way," he said. He felt suddenly tired. This trip to Wilmington was his third road trip this week, and it was only Thursday. It'd be good to start the weekend off early, knowing that he'd just made a score that could leave him sitting pretty for months.

The diner was just off the 40, and midday traffic was roaring by. Donnie leaned on the side of his Subaru, waiting while a heavy truck lumbered by, belching black diesel smoke into the air. When it was gone he told Abigail about the doll and about what it may be worth. He hadn't said anything to Marty about the little dead girl in the picture, or the blood stain on the doll, but he told Abigail.

"Oh God," she said. "That's horrible." A pause. "I bet you took pictures, didn't you?"

He laughed again. "Guilty."

"God, you're a sick man."

"Yeah, but I'm your man."

She huffed. "I suppose that means you have to stop in Raleigh on the way home."

"To see Marty, yeah."

She grumbled under her breath.

"Don't be like he said. She is the expert on this stuff."

More grumbling.

"Don't be jealous. She's not half the woman you are."

"Are you kidding? She's gorgeous."

"Abby, she's got nothing on you."

"You mean like killer legs and big tits? Yeah right, she's got nothing on me."

"Come on," he said.

"Whatever."

"Are you mad at me?"

"No, stupid. Just missing you. Hurry home, okay?"

They said their goodbyes and Donnie hung up. He popped the hatchback and shifted some of the boxes he'd taken from the attic so that the doll wouldn't get any direct sunlight during the car ride to Raleigh. It was a nice June day, very few clouds, and not too hot, but the windows would act like magnifying glass and superheat anything left inside. He'd have to ask Marty for a storage box, he told himself, as he made a little nest for the doll in some of the dresses he'd taken from the attic.

It was then that the little dead girl's picture shifted and slid out from under the clothes beneath the doll, and suddenly her dead face was staring up at him.

Donnie gasped, his breath hitching in his throat.

He stared at the girl, trying to swallow the lump that had formed in his throat, unable to move. His heart was hammering in his chest. For a while, during lunch, the initial unease he'd felt after first encountering the photo had faded and he'd even laughed about it with Abigail on the phone. But now, looking at her picture like this, unexpectedly, he was frozen. So much care had been taken to surround her with dignity, with pious goodwill. But to Donnie, the effect was not kind, not loving, but monstrously misguided and eerie. He could no more leave his gaze upon her than he could upon the sun, and yet he couldn't look away.

Sometime later he became aware of the heat of the sun on the back of his neck.

He shivered and looked around. The parking lot was filling up, the lunch crowd rolling in, though nobody seemed to be paying him much mind.

Donnie looked back at the little dead girl, her straight, oily black hair pulled back over her ears, her little pale hand resting on her belly. He closed his eyes and caught his breath, then cradled his face in his hands and wiped away the cold sweat that had collected there.

He let out a long breath, and threw one of Marianne Staples' dresses over the girl's picture. Then he tossed his iPhone in with his day bag, got in his car, and headed for Raleigh.

* * * * *

Three hours later, he had the doll laid out on the glass coffee table in front of Marty Wright's black leather couch. She sat beside him in a knee-length gray skirt and clingy white top. Their hips were touching. "This is just amazing," she said. She looked stunned. Delighted, but stunned.

"I couldn't believe it either," Donnie said. "Even covered in all that dust I knew it was a Mueller."

"Oh, it's a Mueller all right. There's no question about that." Marty straightened the doll's clothes and whistled. "It's in almost perfect shape. Original clothes. The craftsmanship is simply...there just aren't words. Mueller did such powerful work." She shook her head in admiration. "Wow. Donnie, you hit it out of the park on this one."

"You think so?"

She held his gaze. Out of the corner of his eye, he was aware of how the fabric of her blouse strained at her breasts, at the well-muscled curve of her calves, the strappy sandal dangling from her toes.

He cleared his throat. "Any idea how much it's worth?" he asked.

She sat back and crossed her legs toward him, her sandal dangling inches from his knee. "I think you could take anything you wanted," she said.

He forced himself not to look at her legs. "I told Herb and Frank it might go as high as $130,000."

"Easily," she said. One of her bangs fell down over her face. She let it stay. "I'd have to do a proper prospectus on it before I could tell you for sure, but I bet you could make that the opening bid at auction."

"The opening bid?"

"It'd be a steal at that price."

Donnie swallowed. His face felt hot. His palms were sweating.

"How long would it take you to do that?" he managed to say.

"The prospectus?"

He nodded.

"That depends on how thorough you want me to be?" she said, her voice was a silken purr. Her eyes flashed. She touched his knee. "Certainly overnight."

He looked at her hand. He couldn't stop swallowing. Donnie was happily married, but if he was honest with himself, he didn't know what he'd do if she kept coming on to him like this. It felt like the room was spinning.

"Look, Marty I..."

Unexpectedly, she took her hand away and leaned forward to examine the doll. "The prominence is going to be your problem," she said. Her voice was suddenly clipped, businesslike.

He looked at his knee where her hand had been. "I...what?"

"The prominence," she repeated.

She seemed like a whole different person. It was like she'd flipped off a light switch. Donnie gaped at her, not at all sure what was happening. Was she playing with him? Had he made her mad? He couldn't tell. But she was looking at him now, waiting for him to answer. His mind raced to catch up with what she had just said.

"But, the daughter...we found the doll in her attic." He was babbling. Come on, he thought. Get it together. He said, "I don't understand."

Marty lifted the doll with all the care she would use on a real baby and held it out at arm's length. "So beautiful," she muttered.

"I'm still lost, Marty. What's the problem with the prominence?"

She continued to stare at the doll. "You have no idea what you have here, do you?"

"I...I guess not."

She took the doll over to a stack of white storage boxes and moved boxes around until she found one that fit. She put the doll inside and adjusted its clothes and smoothed its hair, fussed over it like a nervous mother.

"It's a Mueller," she said at last. "That's a sure deal. And it's the cleanest one I've ever seen, too. But if you could show that Mueller made it for his own child, well, then it wouldn't be a rare doll at all, would it?"

"It would be a one of a kind," he said.

"Exactly," Marty said. "Collectors of Mueller's work claim that every doll is made with love akin to magic. I don't know of any other doll maker who inspires that kind of admiration among collectors. They're like a cult. If you could prove that he made this for his daughter, well, there wouldn't be any love greater than that, would there?"

He shook his head.

"And looking at this doll, I can believe what all those collectors have been telling me over the years. I can feel it. Can you feel it?"

The corner of his mouth twitched. "Sure," he said. "Yeah, I feel it."

She brought the doll, now in its box, back to the table and put it in front of him. It stared up at him. Just like a little girl in a coffin, he thought. He shivered, forcing himself to look away from the bloodstain on the doll's cheek.

Marty was beaming at him. Not flirting, but excited, eager. "That doll could be worth millions, Donnie."

He felt like the air had been knocked out of his lungs.

"Millions?" he repeated.

"If you can prove the prominence," she reminded him.

He sat there, his mind reeling with the idea of that much money in his bank account. He and Abigail could pay off the house, buy new cars. He could retire, take her to Venice, London, the Bahamas. Donnie's pulse raced.

Abruptly, his casino eyes cleared and again a darkening unease clouded his mind.

"What is it?" she said. "You okay?"

"Yeah." He looked at the doll again, at the bloodstain. Somewhere in the back of his mind a small voice was telling him to stop, don't go any further, but he forced it down. Millions of dollars, he thought. He said, "What if I told you I had a picture that could prove he made it just for his daughter?"

She huffed. "Then I'd kick you in the knee for not showing it to me the minute you walked in the door."

He tried to smile, but couldn't quite pull it off.

"It's here," he said.

He had a large plastic bin he was using to transport all the stuff from his car up to here. Donnie dug the little dead girl's picture out of that and handed it to Marty.

"That's Sally Staples, I believe. The sister of the woman whose attic I was exploring this morning."

Marty's face blanched. Her lips parted in horrified shock. "This is...dreadful," she said. Her voice was hushed. She closed her eyes. Donnie watched her breasts rise and fall with her breathing. She opened her eyes again, and one hand slowly came up to cover her mouth.

Probably because she's noticed the blood, he thought.

"Marty?" he said.

She extended the picture out to him. "Please take that back," she said. "Put it away. Cover it or something. Please."

"That's why I didn't show the picture right away. I...I knew that..."

He trailed off there, not sure what else he could say. The picture had affected him too. He wasn't surprised that it creeped her out, but he hadn't expected anything as severe as this. Her hand was still over her mouth, but it was her eyes he noticed. They were wet, shining with horror and dismay. He was pretty sure she was about to cry.

"Look, Marty—"

She cut him off with a wave of her hand.

"Just put it away," she insisted.

"Sure. Okay, sure."

He slipped the picture back into the bin and pulled a dress over it. When he turned back to Marty she was over by her desk, taking out a bottle of scotch and a tumbler.

She poured with a shaky hand, the neck of the bottle clanking against the rim of the glass.

Marty sipped her drink. She wouldn't look at him. Her lips were pursed tightly together, like she was trying to keep herself from trembling.

"Marty, we don't have to use this picture. I'm sure there are other ways to prove the prominence."

She put her drink down. She shook her head. "No," she said.

"No?" he said, and waited. Nothing. "Marty, I know this is—"

"No," she said. She looked at him. "No. Take it away, Donnie. I don't want any part of this."

"Marty, don't be—"

"No!" she said. "Take that doll out of here. I won't have any part of this. I won't."

"But, Marty, you said millions..."

"It could be billions, I don't care." She stared at him. "This isn't about money. Do you...do you know what you have there?"

Donnie felt confused by the repeated question. He shrugged. "No, I guess not."

"Donnie, I beg you, take that doll back where you got it. Put it back in that attic with that dead girl's picture and...and..."

She was stumbling over her words, uncertain of what to say.

"But Marty, what's wrong? Talk to me."

"I'm cold," she said. She looked miserable. She shivered, hugging herself. "Donnie, a toy becomes something magic in the mind of a child. We forget that as adults. We grow old and they become objects to us, something our kids love, and that we love because our kids love them. But there's a separation there. Our love is conditional on our children loving them. Do you see? We've changed, not the toys. The toys are the same as when we loved them as kids. They're still magic. It's us. Something inside us ossifies. We get hard, or busy, or callous...I don't know. But we lose something. We forget that toys have power."

He almost smiled. He would have, if she weren't so obviously scared. "Marty, don't you think you're overreacting. I know it's creepy, but, I mean, come on. This is a once in a lifetime score for us."

She shook her head again. "No. No, toys are powerful, Donnie. And dolls are the most powerful of all. A child, a little girl, puts her heart into them. They are the beginnings of motherhood and all the power that goes with that. They become more than toys. It's primal. It's an atavistic thing, Donnie. I think Mueller understood that. In fact, I'm sure he did. I look at that doll, and at the way that dead girl is holding that doll, and I know that Mueller understood the power a doll represents. Call me stupid, I don't care, but I will not have any part of this." She stared at him, eyes burning with emotion. Then her voice softened as she went on: "And Donnie, if you're smart, you won't either."

Donnie didn't know what to say. He looked at her and shrugged.

"Just go," she said. "Please, Donnie. Go. And take all that with you."

"You're serious?"

She nodded.

"Okay," he said. He shook his head. "Marty, I'm sorry."

She scooped up her drink and downed it, her eyes closed. She didn't open them while he packed up the storage bin and made his way to the door. He paused there, waiting for her to say something, to look at him even, but she never opened her eyes.

"Maybe next time," he said, and closed the door behind him as he left.

* * * * *

Two years earlier, while on his fifth road trip in four days, Donnie had been using his iPhone to get directions to a hotel in Harrisburg. There was a convention there, and he was late. It was raining. Morning rush hour traffic. He was trying to figure out what exit to take when his Subaru drifted into the oncoming lanes. There'd been a horn, an 18-wheeler that looked like the side of a building filling up his windshield, and a lucky last second cutback into his own lane. After that he made himself a promise not to use his phone while driving. But his visit to Marty Wright had confused him. Actually, if he was honest with himself, it made him angry. He needed to calm down, to hear a comforting voice. He called Abigail and told her about his visit, leaving out the parts about Marty's dangling sandal and her straining blouse and her hand on his knee. But he told her the rest.

"What do you want to do?" she said.

"About what?" Her question caught him off guard.

"About the doll. Are you going to take it back to Wilmington?"

"It's worth millions," he said.

"That's a lot of money," she said.

"So why would you ask me if I'm taking it back?"

"Donnie, don't snap at me. You called me, remember? Obviously it bothers you, otherwise we wouldn't be talking, right?"

She was right, of course. He was just mad at Marty for making this more difficult than it had to be. Abby didn't deserve this.

"I'm coming home," he said. "Sweetheart, we're gonna be rich."

"I always thought I'd look good married to a rich man."

"You and me both, baby."

* * * * *

He was driving through Greensboro, about ten minutes from home, when his phone rang. It was Herb Cowen's number.

"Hey Herb, what's—"

Donnie was cut off by the sound of something big, like a chandelier, shattering in his ear. The Subaru shimmied as he fumbled the phone. The driver of the beat-to-hell Ford pickup behind him laid on the horn. Donnie flinched. He hated driving. He could be a tiger when it came to auctions. He thrived on the ebb and flow of money, the electric mood of a room in a bidding frenzy. But behind the wheel, amid the ebb and flow of traffic, caught up with other drivers jockeying for position, he often felt rattled, even frightened. He tried to wave an apology to the angry redneck behind him, but the guy would have none of it. The pickup's engine roared as the driver accelerated around Donnie, yelling something that sounded like "Get off the fucking phone, dickhead!" out the window as he surged by.

Donnie watched him go.

Hard, frantic breathing came through the phone. Donnie looked at the phone in surprise. He'd forgotten he was still holding it. He put it back to his ear and listened. There were voices on the other end, panicked voices bulleted by ragged breathing.

"Frank, is that you?"

The voices became inarticulate grunts.

"Frank?"

Donnie heard something thud, and then Frank—he was pretty sure it was Frank; his voice was deeper than Herb's—said something Donnie didn't quite catch.

"Frank? Hey, are you okay?"

No answer. The line was open, but nobody was talking. Maybe he butt-dialed me, Donnie thought. He was about to hang up when he heard something. A small sound, like somebody sobbing.

"Frank, is that you?" He waited a beat. "Herb?"

A car pulled away from the curb just ahead of him. He mashed down on his brakes, his stomach lurching into his throat as the distance to the other car closed at an alarming rate. But he missed it. He waited for the other guy, who didn't wave an apology, Donnie noticed bitterly, turned right at the next corner and slipped away into a neighborhood.

He was still holding the phone, he realized. Enough of this. He hung up and tossed it onto the passenger seat. Focus on your driving, Donnie.

That was it, he told himself as he pulled into his driveway. They butt-dialed me. Had to be. Frankly, he was too tired to assign more meaning to it than that. It had been a long day of driving, of angry rednecks in traffic, of having Marty Wright twist him around her finger like he was made of rubber. He was exhausted. He didn't even want to unpack. He just wanted a shower, maybe some dinner, and then bed. Getting to bed early would be nice.

Abigail greeted him at the back door and helped him bring in the boxes of stuff he'd taken from the attic back in Wilmington. They put it all in his office. She took the lid off the doll's storage box and leaned it up against the backrest of the armchair in the corner of his office. Donnie didn't want to look at it. But Abigail took a step back from it and crossed her arms over her chest, cocking her head from side to side as she studied the doll. "It is beautiful," she said.

He grunted by way of a reply. Standing inside the storage box like that, it reminded him of the Old West outlaws they used to photograph in their coffins along with the men who brought them in.

"Hard to believe somebody would pay millions for it, though."

When he turned to ask her about dinner, she was looking at the picture of the little dead girl.

"This is her?"

He nodded, his lips pressed firmly closed.

"It was a different time, wasn't it?" she said. "Imagine posing your dead child like this. It must have been so painful."

"Yeah. Listen, I'm gonna take a shower, okay?"

"Okay," she said. She put the picture down. "Go take your shower. The steam'll do you good."

And it did, too. Donnie stood under the water, shoulders slumped, feeling tired and depleted.

He toweled off, pulled on a pair of jeans and a ragged Penn State t-shirt, and went out to the kitchen. His nose hadn't completely cleared, but at least he could smell the stew now. He thought he might even be able to stay awake long enough to enjoy it.

Donnie passed through the saloon doors that separated the living room from the kitchen. He expected to see Abigail hovering over her cooking the way she liked to do, but instead saw the dining room table knocked askew, one of the black wooden chairs toppled, and, behind that, Abigail sprawled out on the floor.

"Abigail!"

He rushed to her side and turned her over in his arms.

Her body was stiff as a piece of furniture. But it was the look frozen on her face that caused him to recoil. Abigail's eyes were wide open and staring at something beyond the ceiling. Her mouth was twisted into a scream. A long black lock of her beautiful hair hung over her cheek. Her expression was one of such abject horror and fear that he didn't immediately recognize that she was dead.

"Abigail? No. Oh Jesus, no!"

He scrambled back from her until he ran into the wall and collapsed, his legs stretched out before him. Donnie froze there in panic. For a long moment, he sat staring at her, unable to take it all in. There was no sound but his own taxed breathing. Take her pulse, he thought. CPR, anything. Do something!

He extended a trembling hand toward her, but couldn't make himself touch her. It was too horrible, that look on her face.

Something moved off to his right.

His gaze snapped toward the saloon doors, and his eyes widened. Beyond the doors, a pair of legs. Black shoes. Black stockings. The swish of a black, papery dress.

Donnie shook his head. He pressed his fists into his eyes, as though to grind the vision out, but when he took his hands away, the saloon doors were swinging inward.

He jumped to his feet and ran through the kitchen and into the front parlor. For a moment, the thought that played over and over in his head was: This is where they used to hold funerals, this is where they used to hold funerals—

She was behind him. The little dead girl. He couldn't hear her, but he could sense her. He could feel the dust and the cold gathering at his back, creeping through the sun-bright kitchen, coming for him.

Again he bolted, this time to his office, where he slammed the door shut.

He came to a stop in the middle of the room, staring around at the clutter that came from a lifetime of hunting antiques. The doll, standing like a corpse in its white, casket box, stared back at him with its huge round eyes.

The little dead girl's picture was there, too.

The color fell away from his face. His knees buckled. Her eyes were open, and they were locked on his, vacant and empty, yet somehow weighing him, judging him.

"No," he said. His voice sounded like a sigh. "No."

Lurching back, he turned to flee. But there was nowhere he could go. He realized that like a slap in the face. Donnie thought of the call he'd received from Herb and Frank. It was horror he'd heard in Frank's voice. He knew that now. The same chest-clenching fear that had killed Abigail and put that awful death mask on her face.

And now, the little dead girl was coming for him.

He heard her footsteps on the tile on the other side of the door. It was locked, but he knew that wouldn't matter to her. He knew that just as surely as he knew she'd passed over Marty Wright, spared her because she'd refused to have anything to do with the doll. It was strange to him how clear and reasonable that knowledge was. He knew it was so, knew it just as he knew the little dead girl was coming now for her doll, the one she'd marked with her own blood.

Donnie began to scream. But that didn't last long.

For a moment later, the doorknob creaked and turned, like something long dead groaning back toward life.

I HEARD IT THROUGH THE GRAPEVINE

S. S. Michaels

My footsteps made the carpeted floor sound hollow as I ran along the upstairs hall, glancing over my shoulder. His lopsided footsteps were louder—so loud I thought he'd fall through the stairs, which wouldn't be so bad. I tripped and almost fell and could hear him catching up.

"Daddy," I yelled into my shoulder, "Stop! You're scaring me!"

Heavy uneven stomping. Heavy breathing.

"I'll scare you, you idiotic little shit!"

I turned the corner, scraping my shoulder, and yanked the rope, pulling down the attic steps. He wouldn't follow me up there. He never did. He was afraid his peg leg would get stuck in the ladder rungs. It wasn't really a peg, but one of those metal fake leg things that had a little flipper on the end. He was always getting it caught on something. Plus, one time, I heard him telling Mommy that something happened up there, in our new attic. Something with a box. And music? I don't know what could be so scary about music, but it must have been something really creepy to scare Daddy.

"You'd better not be going in that attic, you little puke!"

Boy, he was really mad this time.

I climbed the rough-hewn ladder and pulled it up behind me, slamming the trap door and engulfing myself in total darkness. Tears burned tracks down my cheeks, my left eye swelling and stinging from where he got me with his belt. I wiped my nose on the sleeve of my Quicksilver hoodie Grandma gave me for Christmas and fumbled for the light bulb. My hand finally closed around the chain and I gave it a quick tug. Washed in the yellowish glow of a sixty-watt bulb, I saw brownish-red streaks lining my gray sleeve. Guess he'd gotten me in the nose, too.

"You rotten little fucker! Come down from there!"

We just moved here a couple of weeks ago. Or maybe a month. Or two months—I'm not too good with time yet. We had to move on account of Daddy's accident at the shop. He needed a different job so we had to move to this side of the state. It didn't matter to me. I didn't have many friends or anything back there. I think Mommy and Daddy don't like it here, though, because everything got real bad here, real fast.

I found the attic one day while Mommy and Daddy were outside talking and drinking with the neighbors. It was a little scary up there at first. Dark, dirty, full of boxes of stuff we didn't use. But, I started going up there when Mommy and Daddy would fight or I'd hear scary noises coming from their bedroom. Pretty soon, I had moved some of the boxes around so I could sit up there and get away from everything and just think or whatever.

I could hear my mommy's muffled voice as I stripped off my hoodie, struggling to keep my t-shirt on. I don't know if Mommy was with me or against me this time. I could never tell which way she was going to go, whose side she'd be on. I guessed *with* from the tone of her far-off voice. I could be wrong, though, 'cause sometimes I am.

"I swear to God, I'll come up there!"

I sat holding my breath, not answering even though there were plenty of things I wanted to yell back at that big jerk. My eye stung so bad.

He wouldn't come up here. The big one-legged chicken.

"I'm going to get the belt again, fuckhead. You know how much it's going to cost me to fix Culverson's window? Asshole!"

Blake, my new friend from down the street, and I had been playing ball in the front yard. Mommy told us it wasn't a good idea, but she never said we couldn't do it. She didn't really care—she was busy talking on the phone to one of her friends from the old neighborhood and drinking a glass of wine. We were using a tennis ball— what could that hurt? Well, I'll tell ya. Blake tossed me a softie and I spanked it good. *Blam!* Right through the Culversons' living room window. Daddy picked just that second to drive up, home from work, his beat-up blue

Dodge Ram slamming to a stop on our cracked driveway. Daddy jumped out and ran around the front end of the truck, catching his little metal flipper in a rut, tripping and scraping his palms on the pavement. Blake took one look at his gaping mouth and furrowed forehead and took off running. He knew what I was in for.

So did I.

After Daddy dragged me over to the neighbors' by my ear and made me apologize, he pulled me into our own house where he whipped off his belt. *Ffffwwwtt*. Right there in the kitchen, he flicked it back, snapped his wrist, and sent it whistling through the air. It connected with my eye, and I guess my nose, too. That's when I turned around and took off running through the house, tearing away from Mommy's grasping fingers. There was one safe place I knew I could go in our new house. And it wasn't Mommy's arms.

It's here, in the attic. The warm, quiet, boxed-in attic.

Daddy's not yelling right now, and I don't hear anything, pressing my ear flat against the rough particle board of the door. I climb over the giant box that has our giant fake pipe-cleaner Christmas tree in it, shove it over the door, and crawl to the other end of the attic. I sit there in my own little space, gently poking at my eye, listening to the quiet punctuated by the occasional thump or thud from two floors below. I wonder what they're doing down there. I wish they'd given me up for adoption, like they say they almost did when they're fighting with each other, which is all the time these days. They know I can hear them—I'm usually right in the same room. They don't care, though.

I don't care anymore, either.

Something hits the latched and barricaded door and I jump like someone poked me with something hot. He won't come up here.

"Hey, fucker, I'm coming for you!"

He says that, but he won't come up. I know he won't. He's too scared of whatever happened that one day, right after we moved in. With the music box or whatever.

Stuff gets quiet again and I settle back against some old moving boxes filled with junk we never unpacked after we moved in. Stuff we used in our old house, fun stuff we used before Daddy got mean and Mommy started drinking wine in the daytime. The Christmas cookie plate we leave out for Santa, all the games we used to play on family game night, Halloween costumes and decorations…

Music.

I hear music.

A very soft, faint Motown sound. (I know what Motown is on account of I've seen it on an infomercial. They had some funny music in the olden days.)

I sit up straight and look around in the gloom. I can't tell where it's coming from. I've been up here a bunch of times, but I don't think there's a radio up here. I guess it could be coming from downstairs, so I settle back with a heavy sigh, crying a little to myself, wishing I was somewhere, anywhere, else. Back at our old house, where no one drank wine or swung a belt. Back at our old house, where I at least had a family.

Something hits the door again and I jump again.

"What, you got that fucking thing locked? There's a lock on that fucking door? You gotta be kidding me. Christ, you think that'll stop me, you little dickhead?"

I hear him stomp away, one-footedly. He won't come up here.

I hope.

The music had stopped but it's started up again. Maybe it's the music Daddy heard that day. This time, it's a little louder. It's definitely not coming from downstairs. Mommy and Daddy don't listen to that kind of music— *"nigger music,"* Daddy called it when we saw the infomercial. Mommy laughed when he said that. I know that's not a nice thing to say. I hate it when Daddy talks now.

I don't want to be here, part of this crazy un-family, in this stupid new house, with these crazy people who hate me. I wish I had a dog. He would love me, protect me from these whacked-out meanies.

I crawl around the dusty floorboards, listening. The music is coming from an old cardboard U-Haul box. One marked with Mommy's name. "Mommy's Old Shit," it says. They think I still can't read, I guess. Or that I don't know what bad words are. Like I don't hear them enough around here.

They don't care.

I press my ear to the box and listen to a snatch of something that might be called "I Heard It Through the Grapevine." Huh? Must be some old radio or something in there.

Then I feel it in my ear—like a hit or a kick from inside the box. A hard one.

I fall backwards and scoot away, crab-style, fast, breathing heavy. What was that? What just hit me in the ear? What the heck is in that box?

I hear something thumping beneath the attic door.

"I'm coming for you, sonny. We're not done talking yet."

He always calls it "talking." Even last month, when I had to have surgery to reset my broken arm, we were just "talking." The doctors had to put screws in my wrist. It's kind of cool 'cause it makes me feel like a cyborg or something, but it makes me sad, too. Makes it kind of hard to use the attic door and carry my school books, too, but I manage.

I creep back over to the box. It's sealed with brown tape. What's in there? I wish I had something sharp to open it with, but I don't. They took away my Swiss Army knife when I carved my name into the old oak in our old backyard. I'd just wanted someone to know I'd been there.

I start picking at one end of the tape and it peels away pretty good. Pretty soon, I have the whole piece ripped off and the top flaps can be lifted open, if I've got the balls.

Pounding on the attic door. Like with a hammer or something.

He's coming up here!

Fuck it. I rip open the box. "I Heard It Through the Grapevine" comes blasting out and I almost pee in my pants. I peek over the edge of the upright flap and find the box is full of old toys and junk: a Rubik's cube, some old action figures, a couple of those pretty pony things girls like to play with, a few Beanie Babies...I'd like to go through this stuff, maybe play with some of it. I mean, it's not all girl stuff. I'm looking at this Star Wars action figure—I think it's Boba Fett, but I'm not sure because I'm not allowed to watch my movies very often—when the top layer of stuff starts to move in a couple of places. It starts, like, sinking down. In rough whirlpools.

I hear a back-and-forth grinding sound. Daddy's sawing the latch off the attic door! I look around for some kind of weapon, but all I see are toys. A plastic unicorn with shiny hair isn't going to do any good.

Then, they erupt from the mess in the box.

Five purplish-brown wrinkled lumps with sunglasses and legs and saxophones.

They're some old action figure things.

And they're *singing*. I am not kidding. They look like…prunes?

I think they're singing raisins. They must have been my mommy's when she was a kid.

I jump back and slam my backbone against a bare upright stud. My teeth clack together and I don't know whether to be more afraid of these singing raisin things or my Daddy coming at me with a saw.

Four little raisin dudes with big white sneakers chicken-walk toward me, pumping their arms, singing. My eyes bug out (well, maybe not the swollen one, but the other one is definitely bugging) and my bladder lets go. Now I feel ashamed on top of just being scared.

I wonder for a second why Mommy kept these things. Then, I think about my grandpa and how he was meaner than Daddy. Or so Mommy says when she's putting the red stinging medicine on my belt scratches, when she's being nice to me.

A loud crash and a cascade of cussing tells me that Daddy's got the attic door off.

The raisin action figure dudes dance in a semi-circle around me.

The attic ladder falls down from the ten-foot ceiling with a slam and a twang of springs, which is followed by more swearing and an angry "ow."

I'm crying now, crouching, rocking back and forth on my heels. Am I losing my mind? I'm only eight. That can't happen 'til you're old, like twenty-two or something, right? I'm okay. I'm okay. I hold my hands on top of my head and repeat to myself that I am okay.

The raisins sing louder, and they spin around all at the same time. I want to scream.

Daddy slides the Christmas tree box away from the doorway. He pokes his head up through the opening, like a prairie dog.

I can't believe he's coming up here!

I squeeze my eyes shut, which hurts, and cover my head with my bony forearms.

I hear the raisins singing and the stomping of Daddy's boot.

"Ha! I told you I'd get you, you little fuck!"

The singing stops and I open my eyes to the most incredible sight. The raisin things are launching themselves at my daddy. One by one, they take running leaps and grab onto his white work shirt—the pocket, the collar. One swings from the end of his blood red tie. Instead of singing now, they're biting!

The raisin action figure dudes are biting my daddy!

And he's screaming and swatting at them. One raisin dude—the one with the big sunglasses—climbs right up Daddy's face and stares him in the eyeball. Daddy hits himself in the nose, missing the little guy, and curses. With a move as smooth as his real low voice, the little raisin plants his mouth on the wet orb of Daddy's eyeball and bites down. Daddy screeches as something wet and greasy leaks down his cheek, in between the raisin's white legs.

Another one of the raisin dudes swings up to Daddy's neck from the very point of his collar. He digs his big white-gloved hands into Daddy's cleanly shaven neck, leaving two tracks of blood as he slides down a couple of inches. I can't see real good, but I think he bites my daddy's neck. Another chomps on his cheek. One hangs on his earlobe. There's lots of blood now, all over Daddy's face and shirt. Daddy sits down hard on the floor, a cloud of dust floating up as his butt hits the boards. He groans and flaps his arms and legs. One raisin cartwheels off of Daddy's flipper, lands on his feet, and bows to me.

I get up, my eye going back and forth between Daddy and the bowing raisin. I make a break for the attic door.

As I climb down the broken ladder, I hear Daddy screaming over "I Heard it Through the Grapevine," which is now my favorite song.

I think I know why Mommy kept those things. I'm going to ask her if I can have them.

She'll probably say no, but I don't care.

DREAMS OF A RAGGED DOLL
Cate Gardner

The ringmaster offered a resounding *NO* that echoed around the ring, stalls and out through the entrance. Anna picked at the stitches running across her wrist. The ringmaster stomped his foot and pointed his gloved hand towards the exit. He couldn't want her to leave. This was her dream. Two clowns approached Anna from either side. They picked her up by her elbows and carried her from the tent. A girl with candyfloss hair and a polished smile sashayed past. Anna didn't think the girl would be right for the circus at all, but then the ringmaster sang *YES* leaving Anna dumbfounded.

Anna pulled her ragdoll, Suzy, from her pocket and picked at the doll's neck stitches. It distracted her from picking at her own. She should have left the doll in its box in the attic; shouldn't have listened to it.

"If you carry on doing that, my head will fall off. You don't want that," Ragdoll Suzy said.

Ragdoll Suzy had orchestrated the audition piece—the real girl who became a doll. They'd sat in the attic all night threading cotton through Anna's skin, covering every joint and crease and making seams along her arms, legs and torso.

Anna forced all the air from her body and flopped forward, her arms drooping between her legs, her fingers drifting through grass. A clown-shaped shadow swept over her. Anna's spit drooled on the clown's shiny shoes. His still burning cigarette brushed through her hair; tiny sparks flickered and died.

The mournful clown stared at her, his downturned smile both painted and real. He shook his head. Anna straightened her back causing several of the stitches running down her spine to tear.

"You shouldn't fuss so," the clown said, words that had infected her childhood.

A sob built in her chest. How to explain to this man who was dressed in oversize shoes, red nose and curly green wig that she was nothing without a dream. She reached into her pocket for a handkerchief. Instead, the folded recruitment flyer for *The Drim & Drab Circus Troupe* fluttered out. They should have said yes. Anna fussed with Ragdoll Suzy's hair. The doll blinked but didn't betray her animation by speaking in front of the clown. Suzy had not been so shy beneath the rafters when persuading Anna to pull her from the cardboard box.

"If I leave my dream will be done," Anna said.

Squeals echoed from within the tent. Sounded like the Ringmaster. Yet, she couldn't stay; each giggle, every delighted word tugged and unravelled a stitch. The clown bowed his head. Perhaps he did understand what it meant to watch a dream die. Perhaps this was her one and only circus performance. She hung her head lower to offer him a decent show, and then she turned and shuffled away, feet dragging through soil, the exit seeming an impossible distance.

"Quitter," Ragdoll Suzy said. "If I had bones, they'd have picked me."

The clown followed them across the sunburned grasses, out through the rusted park gates and under the railway bridge. Luminous graffiti lit the dark...*Dreams Die Here*. Ragdoll Suzy giggled. The clown's breath tickled the back of Anna's neck. Leaving the dark of the bridge, she pressed her hand to her eyes and waited for the sun's glare to lessen. The clown pressed against her back. When she perched on a bollard outside the transport café, the clown perched on the neighboring bollard.

Anna picked at stitches running from thumb to wrist and unravelled three. Her chest felt as if it would burst from the fight to contain her loss. The clown pulled a string of moth eaten handkerchiefs from his yellow jacket and held them out to her. She tried to grab one, but her hand passed through it.

Not real. The clown looked even more mournful at the fact. He opened his mouth to object, but no words exited and he faded.

"In not recognizing him, you killed his dream," Ragdoll Suzy said.

Anna recalled him now; a squat clown, stuffing imploding from his belly, buried amid old toys in a box bound for the attic. A tear trickled down her cheek, catching on a stitch end. She knew saying '*he was just a toy*' wouldn't cut it. Sometimes she thought the world a toy box, and that nothing was real, that someday a hand would delve in and throw her into the trash, which was pretty much how she felt today.

She unpicked several more stitches until she'd unravelled her skin up to her elbow. A lorry hissed into the parking lot and the lorry driver hopped out the cab. He looked as sprightly as a trapeze artiste. Crossing the lot, he spat on the tarmac and ran a hand through his greasy hair. Anna followed him into the café. Bacon fat sizzled and coffee brewed, determined to prove that the world was real.

By the time the driver had ordered breakfast, Anna had unravelled her left arm from elbow to shoulder. Ragdoll Suzy stretched her lips to form a black hole O. Blood pooled on the table. Anna stuffed napkins into the shoulder socket to stem the flow. Sawdust mingled with the blood, proving that the circus did run through her veins. The driver sat at the adjacent table. He stared at her between bites of toast, bacon and egg. She took the flyer from her pocket and placed it on his table. Her left arm hung from a single thread. The driver gagged, toast lodged in his throat.

"Do you have a dream? If not, we could form a partnership. Your lorry would look mighty fine stuffed with carnival tents." She waited a moment, and when he didn't answer, she added, "Please. Without a dream I am nothing."

The driver pressed his hand to his mouth and ran in the direction of the toilets. Spying his keys sitting beside his plate, Anna palmed them and left the café. She'd never driven a lorry before and suspected attempting to drive one handed would be difficult. Grabbing the side of the cab with her good arm, Anna hoisted herself into the lorry.

She stabbed the key into the ignition, fired the engine and just sat there. In the wing mirror, she watched the driver exit the café. He carried Ragdoll Suzy.

Anna bit the stitches securing her lower lip. Having crossed the forecourt, the driver reached up and pulled her good arm. It unravelled at the elbow. Anna dropped from the cab before she lost the arm. Ragdoll Suzy lay grinning beside her.

"Freak," the driver said, knocking her aside and wiping his hands down his jeans.

"I just wanted to belong to them."

She wished her clown would return holding a festoon of paper flowers and a letter of recommendation. She should have stolen him from the attic and not Ragdoll Suzy. He could have taught her how to tumble, how to make folk laugh. Anna scooted along on her bum, rolled over and used her knees to help her stand. She'd try the circus again. Be someone else. Anna pulled at her elbow stitches and reaffixed them as best she could. The blood had already begun to clot.

"I wouldn't leave me behind again," Ragdoll Suzy said.

With hope dented and worn, but not beyond repair, Anna bent and picked up Suzy, then headed back to the circus. A jaunty melody echoed across the park drawing in the punters. The candyfloss haired girl manned the entrance, handing out tickets and hypnotizing passers-by with her teeth. Anna wished she could sew the girl's lips together. She was sure Suzy would agree. The doll hung limp from Anna's fingers, playing toy.

"It's five pounds to enter," the candyfloss girl said, grabbing Anna's elbow. Stitches tore.

"I'm a circus artiste," Anna said.

In her hand, Ragdoll Suzy's chest moved as if Suzy fought to contain her snort.

"Oh wait, didn't I see you at the auditions? Go ahead, I won't tell anyone you didn't pay."

"It was my dream to be here, was it yours?"

The girl's eyes widened. All she could muster was, "Sorry."

Anna loped towards the audition tent, her left ankle threatening to snap beneath the weight of broken dreams. They wouldn't say no this time. With her arms hanging from tenuous threads, she was too freakish for them to reject. She looked at her chest, concerned the stitches above her heart had loosened; her chest ached with the want of this place. Drawing in a sawdust breath, Anna entered the tent. It took a moment for her eyes to adjust to the dark. The tent had emptied, the ringmaster returned to his caravan before the show, the clowns to their dressing rooms. Only empty seats, elephant dung and abandoned recruitment flyers remained.

Anna dropped to the floor, knee stitches snapping. If the ringmaster and his clowns came back now, surely they'd see her act worth investing in. And her upkeep costs were low—needle and thread. Her head dipped forward, too heavy for her neck. Ragdoll Suzy dropped from Anna's fingers and stood with no bend to her rag limbs. Anna's head continued to droop, dragging at stitches, exposing her spine.

Outside the tent, a barker shouted, "Roll up, roll up."

More stitches popped. Anna dragged herself to the seats and crawled beneath them. Ragdoll Suzy remained in the center of the ring, cracking knuckles she hadn't had until a moment before and testing the strength of a newly grown spine. Anna stared out at the ring, too floppy and unravelled to crawl back into the show. The ringmaster entered, followed by eager customers. People filled the seats. Wood creaked above Anna's head while she peered from between someone's swollen ankles. Center stage, Ragdoll Suzy bowed and even the Ringmaster offered a gasp.

"My dream," Anna whispered. "You've stolen my dream." No one heard her.

Ragdoll Suzy hopped onto a clown's shoes and addressed the audience, "Everyone has dreams and in places like this, some of them come true."

"Sensational," the crowd agreed and broke the last of Anna's stitches with their applause.

ATTIC DOG
David Raffin

The attic dog is old. He is one of the first of his kind. His circuits are integrated. He has integrity. His power source is corroded, and depleted. He is powerless. He is corrosive. He lives in your house. He gets around. You never know where he will be found. Except somewhere in the attic, definitely.

He often lies on discarded remnants of shag carpet. They are a bright orange shag remnants and he is a short faux-brown haired dog; he himself is not shaggy. Because he is both powerless and corroded, he has no bark preceding his bite.

The attic is a mess. No one remembers the dog is there.

There is a box of old crackerjack prizes in the attic. Mostly small books that came with small magnifying glasses. The magnifiers have been long lost. All that remain are the small books, filled with small jokes. They provide levity to the dog. They also provide frustration, due to the eyestrain.

There is a box filled with old horror movies on VHS tape. They are large. The boxes are extra roomy for the tape contained within. The tape within is cradled either by a thin black plastic pull-out container or an even more awkward thick corrugated cardboard pull-out unit. They are fillers. The boxes have disquieting pictures of things like axe murder. This does nothing for the dog's sense of security. The dog can only speculate as to the actual content of the tapes, there being neither VCR or television in the attic. The whole situation serves to confound the dog.

There is a box filled with old paperbacks on the subject of UFOs and ESP. The dog has read them. The dog knows how to set fires with its mind. There is also a VHS box that details this. It does not seem like a good idea to the dog at this time. He does, however, understand that knowledge is power. There might come a time. There might yet come a time.

There is a rubber chicken in the attic. The dog finds this in bad taste.

There is a marmalade jar filled with volcanic ash— with masking tape on it and a childish script stating: "Volcanic ash, 1980."

There is a Tupperware container filled with oil paint and mold, dated 1982.

There is a container filled with old rusty nails and screws, undated.

There are beaten and battered board games—taped, and yellowed with age.

There is a coloring book filled with anthropomorphic dogs wearing hats and vests but no pants. There is a velvet painting of dogs playing pool.

Mostly the dog does not know what to make of it. Sociologically, it is a mish-mash.

There is a book detailing physics. The dog knows how to split atoms. It is a theoretical understanding, unlike the aforementioned ability to start fires. He lacks proper equipment. And opposable thumbs. While he has mastered pyrokinesis he is still working on telekinesis. If he had access to the equipment he would have the means.

The dog has time. Plenty of time.

There is a box of broken clocks and wristwatches.

The dog cannot figure out how to work the latch on the door. One day. One day.

The dog has set up a system of booby-traps. To deal with intruders. The dog guards.

This is the dog's domain. He is master over all.

There is a monster making machine. It makes spiders and scorpions from gelatinous goo in metal plates. There are various beasts throughout the attic. The dog made some of them. The ones that he has made he has named. The ones that he did not make chose their own names or go nameless.

The nameless ones cannot be trusted.

It is neither day or night in the attic, though the spiders argue that it is always night in the absence of day.

The dog is not one for sophistry. He is literal minded. He was made that way. He is straight forward.

The dog cannot walk backwards. However, before his batteries were corroded, he could flip.

The rubber spiders hate the live spiders but the live spiders are without opinion regarding the rubber spiders.

The dog considers them the same though he knows they are not the same.

The dog has the head of an action figure he carries with him. It is the head of the Six Million Dollar Man. He uses the bionic eye in the head of the action figure to read the miniaturized joke books that still smell of decades old Crackerjack.

The dog makes due.

The dog has chewed the heads off every doll or action figure in the attic. He has melted the bodies with his mind. He has used their plastic to make more spiders and scorpions. These are the hard ones. They are not flexible in body or spirit. He has mounted the heads of the action figures awkwardly on the spiders and scorpions.

There is a globe and a world encyclopedia in the attic and the dog has explored it from cover to cover to cover, repeatedly. This way, the dog has seen the world. The world he has seen is from 1955.

The dog worries about the cold war.

The dog wonders if there is anything beyond the attic.

The dog works hard to create a new and better world.

A world without humans. A world with plastic and rubber spiders, some with the heads of the extinct race of man. A world without the evils of VHS. A world where all the jokes are writ large. A world where he alone is the master of fire and the atom, for he alone can be trusted with this mighty burden. A world where a dog can get a thorough brushing and a new battery every so often. An ideal world. A utopia. A dog's world.

Something to flip over, again.

WHEN HARRY KILLED SALLY
Lisa Morton

Melissa stood in her nine-year-old daughter's bedroom, staring down at the toy wreckage. "Sharona, what happened here?" She motioned at a headless doll; from its dress, she recognized it as Sally, a strange little patchwork figure that had been one of Sharona's favorites.

The little girl shrugged and kept playing a loud and annoying videogame on her PlayStation. "She had a fight with Harry. They broke up. He killed her again."

"Harry? You mean the teddy bear?"

Sharona grunted agreement, and Melissa sighed. *Nine years old, and she's still mutilating dolls, except now it's after they've had a bad break-up. We've spent money on every kind of therapy, medications, special schools…*

Melissa knelt, found the decapitated doll's head under the bed, and retrieved it. The head had not only been ripped off, but half the hair had been yanked out, giving the doll the appearance of a cancer patient. *What on earth possesses her to DO this? None of my friends have kids who destroy everything.*

There was no sign of the marauding teddy. "Where's Harry?"

"He went to the attic."

"Sharona…honey, we've talked about this before. You know I don't want you going up to the attic by yourself." Their house, a 1940s bungalow, had an attic that was little more than a crawlspace and could only be reached by setting up a ladder beneath an opening in the hallway, but somehow Sharona kept finding her way up there. "That ladder's too big for you, and besides, there are probably all kinds of nasty molds and spiders up there—"

Sharona cut her mother off. "I didn't say I went up there. I said Harry did."

"Oh, I see. So how did he get up there, then?"

No answer. Sharona pretended to focus on her game.

Melissa wanted to unplug the goddamn PlayStation right then and there, force her daughter's attention for once...but all the psychiatrists and specialists had cautioned against displays of anger. "Sharona's a very special child," they'd say. The school officials all used that same phrase, whenever they talked about Sharona's problems with her classmates—how their books had been tampered with, or their pencils snapped. *Special child.*

But I don't want this kind of special, Melissa had been tempted to respond.

She decided to check the attic instead, to see if the bear really was there. Maybe she'd have a better handle on how to deal with her temperamental, willful child if she knew whether she was telling the truth.

She found the ladder in the garage (*how did a nine-year-old lug this thing back and forth?*), carried it into the hallway, unfolded it beneath the trap door and climbed up. The trap pushed up easily, and Melissa stepped up further. The attic was gloomy, late afternoon sunlight slanting in through a few vents, picking out dust motes in the stale air. There was a bare bulb overhead, and Melissa's groping fingers found the dangling pull chain. Light flooded the space, and she saw boxes of old clothing, Christmas decorations, some broken furniture—

And a pile of toys. Not just Harry, the small stuffed brown bear, but also a Barbie, a plush Tweety, and a little pink toy car she didn't remember ever seeing before.

Why would she put all of these in the attic? Must've been one big doll rumble.

Harry had been a big, sweet-faced, stuffed bear—a custom-made one that'd cost a small fortune—but for some reason looking at the thing now sent a shiver up Melissa's back. Had it always had that smirk at the corner of the sewn-on mouth? Or maybe it was the way it seemed to have one foot on the Barbie, like a conqueror crushing a villager underfoot.

Forcing her unease aside, Melissa gathered the toys in one arm and climbed down with the other. She was about to pull the trap shut when she heard something: a skittering across the rough boards that made up the attic's floor.

Oh, great…now we have rats?

She cautiously poked her head up again—and was startled to find herself inches from a grinning, bug-eyed face. Melissa jerked back in shock, banging her neck on the rim of the opening, then she forced her heart to slow down as she realized what she was looking at: it was another of Sharona's toys, a big green ogre thing.

How did I miss seeing that before? Melissa hesitated—she didn't like the thought of touching the ogre any more than Teddy—before reaching out and adding the doll to her armload.

Back in Sharona's room, she set all the retrieved toys down on the floor. Sharona glanced over briefly, then said, "Should've left 'em in the attic. There's gonna be trouble now."

Melissa thought there already was.

* * * * *

That night, Melissa was still awake at 2 a.m., her husband Nelson snoring softly beside her. She stared into the darkness, her thoughts forever circling back to her daughter.

We did everything right. We followed all the guides. We fed her the right things, bought her every toy, hired nannies and tutors, but nothing worked. She should have been the perfect child. But she's not even what my sisters all have.

Her thoughts were interrupted by a rapid series of creaks from overhead. Something was in the attic.

What…?

A cat. Or maybe a possum. She'd seen one of those ugly rodents out by the trash last week. *Were they rabid? Would it attack Sharona if she tried to climb up there again?* In the morning she'd set the ladder up and take look.

* * * * *

She found Harry in the attic again.

73

There was no sign of any animal, no opening she could see where one could have gotten in…but there was Sharona's bear.

Somehow the bear looked…different. Its glass eyes seemed wild, the brown fake fur somehow puffier, as if an electrical current had run through it. Melissa had to force herself to pick it up, and then she held it away from her body.

She took off from work early so she could pick up Sharona from school; as usual, her child walked alone, away from all the other happy third-graders who strode off in groups of two or three.

"Sharona," Melissa asked, after their seatbelts were fastened, "did you crawl back up to the attic last night and put Harry there again?"

"Harry attacked Sally again and I told him he was very bad. She's tired of being killed."

Melissa forced herself to stay calm. "Honey, that doesn't answer my question."

Sharona made an exasperated sound, then said, "He and the ogre keep beating up on the other dolls."

The shrinks had all warned her that "special children like Sharona" frequently used dolls as stand-ins for their own hostility, but Melissa had to bite back on her own frustration now. "They're just toys, Sharona. They don't attack each other."

Sharona shrugged. "Try telling them that."

* * * * *

Melissa locked up the ladder. She found an old bicycle cable and lock in the garage, and used them to secure the ladder to Nelson's table saw.

Let's see you get to the attic NOW, Harry.

* * * * *

That night she heard the clattering sound overhead again. The next morning she unlocked the ladder, crawled up into the attic, and saw Harry and the ogre waiting near the opening.

Harry still had a small pink plastic arm clenched in one fluffy fist.

Later that day she found Mrs. Hernandez, the babysitter/housekeeper who came in during the afternoons before Melissa got home, and asked her if she knew anything about someone going up to the attic.

"Attic? No," answered the nanny in her thick Salvadorean accent. Melissa still wasn't entirely sure she trusted the woman, but she was the only one they'd found who'd put up with Sharona's tantrums, and she was affordable, too.

At dinner, Melissa told Nelson something was going on. "Sharona's putting things in the attic."

Nelson snorted mashed potatoes, then wiped his mouth. "Is that a euphemism for something?"

"No. She's mutilating her toys, then she puts them in the attic."

Nelson grunted. "So?"

Melissa huffed in exasperation, then said, "You don't find that a little odd?"

"She's a kid. They do weird shit."

Nelson excused himself to work on a report that was due in the morning. Melissa checked in on Sharona, and asked if everything was okay.

"God, Mom, stop with the interrogations, okay?!"

* * * * *

Early in the morning, Melissa awoke when she heard not only skittering sounds—like tiny footsteps—from the attic, but a small voice as well. This time she wasn't going to wait; she flew out of bed and ran down the hallway. There was no sign of the ladder, but she could still hear the overhead noises. She also heard chattering from Sharona's room.

She didn't knock, but instead threw back her daughter's door and flipped on the overhead light.

Sharona sat on the floor by her bed, surrounded by toys...all of which were damaged in some way. Sally was nothing now but a plastic torso with a dress; Barbie had an arm sticking out of her neck-stump. Teddy and the ogre were noticeably missing.

"Sharona, what is going on?!"

When the little girl looked up, Melissa nearly flinched from the sheer viciousness on the small face. "They were *very* bad this time."

"How?" Melissa didn't have to check the attic; she knew she'd find the missing toys there. "How are they getting up there?"

Sharona shouted, "Just leave me alone! I hate you!"

"I'm not leaving you alone, Sharona! Tell me how they get up there NOW!"

Sharona's features abruptly twisted into a feral grin. "Okay, Mommy."

Melissa's vision went black. It took her a few seconds to realize that she was on her knees and couldn't move. She smelled the dust and mildew of the attic.

The dusty bulb overhead clicked on, and Melissa saw her daughter seated a few feet away, still baring her teeth. And the toys were there—Teddy and the ogre and a few more—and they were walking slowly towards Melissa, on feet made of rubber and plastic and stuffed fur. Melissa struggled, but some force held her in an iron grip.

"Sharona," Melissa managed through a locked jaw, "are you...?"

The toys advanced. Sharona giggled.

She was a very special child.

LIVING DOLL

Piers Anthony

Tumble was ready to call it a day. His late grandfather's attic was crowded, stale, and hot, and he had been slowly cleaning it out for hours. His folk were cleaning up the house for sale, and naturally Tumble, the clumsy one, got the wearing but safe job. Which was all right; he knew he wasn't much of a person, and he was satisfied to do the best he could. It was sad, though, because he had liked the gruff old man, and was sorry for this evidence of his demise.

There was a small stout wooden chest before him. Very well, he would check that out, then get out of the oppressive heat.

He unlatched the lid and lifted it. Inside was a doll. What was Grandpa doing with anything like this? He had been no girly-man, but a tough old buzzard. The only dolls he liked were the living kind.

It certainly was lovely. It looked to be anatomically correct, garbed in a hula skirt and halter that showed a phenomenal shape, with a pretty face and massive dark hair that extended to her plush bottom.

Curious, Tumble lifted the doll out of her case. She was about a foot tall and perfect in every detail. "I wish I had a girl like you," he breathed. Of course even the wish was foolish. Girls knew him for what he was, an awkward oaf, and stayed well away. Even if he had one like this, she would soon depart for some better man.

The doll shimmered. She expanded rapidly. In a moment she stood before him, his hand on her petite waist, her hand cupping his. "Your wish is my command," she said.

Amazed and embarrassed, he sought to jerk away his too-familiar hand. But she held on to it. "Don't do that! You have to keep touching me, or I will revert to doll status. Do you understand?"

"No," he said candidly. Then, so she would know he wasn't trying to insult her, he explained: "I'm not the brightest candle on the chandelier. I don't know who you are or why you came here or how you relate to the doll."

She smiled, and he could have sworn the dark attic brightened. "Tell me your name, and I will tell you mine, and clarify things for you."

"I'm Tumble, because—"

"I get it, Tumble. You must have fallen a few times as a child, so they hung a cruel nickname on you, and it stuck."

"Uh, yeah."

"I am Epiphany. I am a woman enchanted to become a doll in my own image. I can resume my natural aspect only when being touched by a man. When he stops touching me, I revert, and am dead to the world. So I am holding your hand not from excess of passion, though I can provide that when requested, but to be sure we can have a dialogue long enough to clarify my nature."

"Uh, yeah," he repeated uncertainly.

"Do you have any questions?"

"Yeah, I do. What are you doing here in Grandpa's attic? He wasn't exactly a doll man."

"Ah, you are Trevor's grandson. There is a family resemblance."

"Yeah. Except he was ten times as smart as me, for one thing."

"To answer your question, I was servicing your grandfather. He took me out when he was horny, and put me back when sated."

Tumble was appalled. "He treated you like a—a—"

"Exactly. I must obey the man who touches me, and that was his interest, especially when he became a widower."

Tumble realized he was blushing. "I'm sorry, Miss Epiphany. I didn't know."

"Don't be concerned. I was enchanted in significant part for this purpose, and I'm good at it. I am the ultimate sex toy. It's not a burden to me. I have known many men over the course of decades, and Trevor was by no means the worst of them. But now you must do what he did not: return me to my mistress."

"Oh sure, Miss Epiphany. Who is she?"

"Call me Pip for short. She is the Sorceress of Bleak Mountain. Surely you know of her."

"Oh, yeah, Miss—Pip. She does our village a lot of good, but we are careful not to trespass on her mountain. Only the folk with regular business go there, like the ones bringing vegetables, meats, leather, and the housemaids, who never see her, but they do their jobs and get away quickly. In return she gives us good rains and good crops, and we don't want to mess with her."

"That is a good attitude. Had she known that I was being used by your grandfather, she might not have been so kind to your village. But I'm sure she'll forgive all, if you take me promptly back."

"Right away," Tumble agreed. But privately he wondered what the Sorceress would want with a sex toy.

She gazed at him a moment. "Perhaps tomorrow will do. It seems to be late in the day."

"Yeah. What should I do, put you back in your box, then fetch it in the morning?"

"Tumble, I am just a bit tired of the box. Take me with you downstairs."

"But then everyone will see you, and maybe not let you go, because you must be pretty valuable."

"More than you know," she agreed, smiling. "But do not be concerned. Only you can see or hear or feel me, when I am animate, and when I am not, I am just an inert doll. Just hold my hand and go down."

"Oh, yeah, I guess, if that's the way you want it."

"That's the way it is."

They went downstairs. She was so light and balanced that her dainty feet hardly seemed to touch the steps.

"'Bout time you came down, Tumble," his mother said, spotting him. "Wash your hands; supper's almost ready."

"Sure, Ma," he agreed, as he always did. Epiphany was right beside him, holding his hand, but his mother seemed not to see her.

"I told you there would be no trouble," Epiphany said. Or hear her. "Yeah."

But his mother heard that. "What's that, Tumble?"

"Nothing, Ma. I was just talking to myself."

"Don't do that. It makes a bad impression."

"She's right," Epiphany said as he walked toward the bathroom. "Do not speak aloud to me when you are in company. Just ignore me."

He glanced at her beside him, and accidentally saw down inside her halter. He blushed as he snapped his eyes away. "That's sort of hard to do."

She laughed. "You'll learn. No need to sneak peeks, either; just tell me to take off my clothes, and I will." She drew down her halter, exposing her breasts completely. They were phenomenal.

"No!" he exclaimed. "I'm not supposed to look! Girls don't like to be goggled."

"Ogled," she corrected him. "But I'm not like that. My body is yours any time you want it."

"Oh no, no, no! I wouldn't—" He could hardly contain his acute embarrassment.

She squeezed his hand. "I see. You have no experience with women."

"Yeah. I don't know what to say to them or anything."

"How old are you, Tumble?"

"Nineteen. Past time for me to find a job and contribute to the family."

"And to marry?"

He shrugged. "If I ever find a woman who'll have me."

"For that you need experience. Which for you is hard to get. Perhaps we can do something about that tonight." She lifted her halter and was decently covered again.

Was she teasing him? He dared not ask. They were in the bathroom now, and she helped him wash his face and hands, never letting go.

He had a normal supper. No one saw Epiphany as she sat on his lap and kept a hand on his upper arm. For that matter, they hardly saw Tumble. He was pretty much ignored, as usual.

But after the meal, when he was washing the dishes—another chore that fell naturally to him, since he wasn't good for much else—his mother broached him. "Tumble, what's going on?"

She had caught on that he was up to something, as she always did. What could he tell her?

"Tell her the truth," Epiphany suggested.

That made it easier. "I found something in the attic today."

She smiled tolerantly. "That's hardly surprising. There's a lifetime of your grandfather's junk there."

"A toy. In fact a doll. A beautiful doll. And—"

"And?"

"Tell her," Epiphany said.

"And it came to life, sort of."

His mother's eyes narrowed. "Perhaps I should see this doll."

Her "perhaps" was his command. But this was awkward.

"You will have to set me down," Epiphany said. "For a moment. Then animate me again after she has seen."

"Uh, yeah." She was holding on to his arm. He put his other hand on her arm and moved it to the counter, then let go.

Epiphany disappeared. The doll appeared, lying on her back on the counter.

"Oh, my!" his mother breathed. "That's it!"

This was unlike her. "That's what?"

She did not answer directly. "Tumble, when you touched her, and she came to life, what did she do?"

"She talked to me. Said Grandpa had used her, but she needed to be returned to the Sorceress of Bleak Mountain. So that's what I'll do."

"What else?"

"Else?" he asked, confused.

"What else did she do with you?"

"She—" He blushed. "She showed me her breasts. She sure is pretty."

"And?"

"She said I needed experience. But I know that's not right. I mean, not with a doll."

"So you didn't do anything else with her."

"Yeah. Did I do right?"

"Yes." But her mouth was tight. "Tumble, you must not do anything more with her. That doll is hazardous."

"She sure seemed nice."

"Here is the story," she said grimly. "Legend has it that when the Sorceress was eighteen years old, and the most beautiful woman of her generation, she made a doll in her own image so there would always be a record of her beauty. It was a magic doll, said to come alive when touched by a man, and to oblige him in any manner he chose. That meant only one thing, men being what they are. But someone stole the doll, and the Sorceress was so angry that when it wasn't promptly returned she turned Bleak Mountain into a volcano that erupted and killed the entire village beside it. Later our own village was founded, and the Sorceress has taken good care of us. But we have known not to try her patience. We didn't know this doll was here. You must return it tomorrow, with our abject apology, and hope the Sorceress is not angry."

"I'll do that," he said, shaken.

"Do not do anything with it that might annoy the Sorceress. She is phenomenally dangerous when angry. Do you understand?"

"Yeah, I think so. Don't use her the way Grandpa did."

"That's it. Best not to touch it at all. We can wrap it in cloth for you to carry."

"But she said to animate her again, after I showed you. I said I would."

His mother winced. "Oh, damn! It's a trap."

"A trap?"

"If you don't touch her, and return her wrapped, the doll may be angry, and will tell the Sorceress that you molested her, and there will be an almost literal hell to pay. But if you animate her again, she'll seduce you, and that may also annoy her mistress. We're damned either way."

"But she seems so nice! And she knows I'm just trying to do the right thing."

"You always try to do the right thing, Tumble. But sometimes it can be difficult to know what is right."

"Yeah."

"All right. Animate her, but don't use her. Tell her what I said, and hope she is reasonable."

"Yeah." He put his hand on the doll's arm.

Epiphany manifested immediately. "No need to tell me, Tumble. I heard."

"You're not mad?"

"I'm not mad. Your mother is a good woman. Tell her I said I'd treat you right."

"Pip says she heard, she's not mad, and will treat me right," Tumble relayed.

"You're talking to her now?"

"Yes. I know you can't see her, but she's right here. We're holding hands."

"So she can hear me."

"I can," Epiphany agreed.

"She can."

His mother faced where she judged Epiphany to be. "My son's a good boy. He wants to do what's right. But he doesn't always know what's right. Please, if you have any conscience, let him deliver you safely to the Sorceress, and tell her the truth about what happened here. We didn't know the old man was keeping the doll. I beg you, as a loving mother."

"I can't swear to that," Epiphany said. "But I can tell you this: neither I nor the Sorceress wishes you or your village any ill. We shall see how it resolves."

Tumble relayed her words. His mother relaxed only slightly. "Then we shall simply have to hope for the best."

"Yes." Epiphany leaned forward and kissed her on the cheek.

"Oh! I felt that!"

"I can make others feel me when I try," Epiphany agreed. Then she turned to Tumble. "Time for bed, I think."

"Bed," he agreed.

His mother winced again, but did not comment.

Tumble returned to his bed under the eves. They were staying in his grandfather's house while they shaped it up for sale, and this was where there was room for him. But he hesitated to strip to his underclothing, because of Epiphany's presence. "Maybe I should let you be the doll, for the night."

"Oh, no you don't. I've been asleep for so long I want to live a little. I'll share your bed."

"But—"

"Your mother's afraid I'll seduce you."

"Yeah." It would hardly be difficult; her very presence aroused him painfully.

"And that will anger the Sorceress."

"Yeah."

"Let me make this clear, Tumble. If you force yourself on me, my mistress will be angry. But if I choose to seduce you, she won't. She just doesn't like me to be abused."

Tumble was sorely tempted, but wary. No girl had ever made such an offer, let alone as ravishingly lovely a one as this. But was it right? He was pretty sure his mother would not think so. "I wish Grandpa could advise me now."

"You were close to him?"

"Sometimes. At least he taught me three things."

"Oh? What are they?"

"First, to appreciate beauty wherever I might find it. Second, how to fight off thugs. Third, always to do the right thing. He said the third is where he failed, but with luck I'd be a better man."

"I think Trevor knew you'd find me."

"Maybe. I'll sure try to do what he said."

Epiphany considered, then brought her face close to his. "Trevor gave you good advice. I will try to let you follow it."

"That's nice," he said uncertainly. "I was afraid you were going to kiss me."

She laughed. "I *am* going to kiss you. Then I will leave you alone for the night, except for maintaining our contact so I won't revert."

"But if you kiss me, I'll—" He couldn't say what, because her very nearness was stirring his emotions phenomenally.

"You'll sleep. This time. That's part of my magic."

"I don't know. If—"

She kissed him. He felt as if he were floating to the ceiling.

Then it was morning, and he woke refreshed after dreaming endlessly of that kiss. He feared he loved her already. Had she bewitched him?

She seemed to read his thought. "No, Tumble, I merely put you to sleep. Your own nature did the rest. You are a healthy young man with a normal appreciation of the feminine form."

"I guess you could have, if you'd wanted."

"Yes, I could have seduced you, and I did want to, but I'm trying to play fair. I'm giving you your chance to deliver me to my mistress. But I can't guarantee my future behavior."

"Thanks, I guess."

She laughed. "We'll see."

After breakfast they set off for Bleak Mountain, which was not far, but the path was rugged. It would be a half day's walk.

Unfortunately two village toughs were passing by. When they saw Tumble, they cut across to intercept him.

"Oh, darn," he muttered. "Pip, I'm going to have to let go of you, because I'll need to deal with these bullies. Otherwise they'll take you, and you'll never get home."

"I can do a little enchantment, enough to mess them up long enough for you to pass."

"No, thanks, I should handle my own problems, if I can."

"As you prefer."

He brought out his handkerchief and took hold of her other arm, then let go of her hand. She reverted to doll form. He held her close to his chest and walked on.

They stood athwart the path, blocking his way. "Hey Tummy Dummy!" one said. "Whatcha got there? You playing with dolls now?"

"I have to return it to the Sorceress."

They peered closer. "That's some doll! Looks sexy as hell. Look at those gams! We'll take it."

"No."

"We don't much like that word, Dummy. We're asking you nice. Hand it over or we'll pound you."

"No."

The bullies smiled. Now they had a pretext to pound him. One reached for Tumble while the other reached for the doll.

Tumble's left hand was free. He swung it forward and out, suddenly and hard. The knuckles of his fist cracked into the bully's face so hard that blood spattered. Then Tumble ducked down and launched his right shoulder into the gut of the other. The air went out of him and he went down, gasping helplessly.

Tumble walked on. After a moment he touched the doll.

Epiphany appeared. "You weren't fooling about handling thugs!"

"Yes, when I have to. It's only the one thing, that I have drilled on hundreds of times, so I'm not clumsy."

"But they'll be lurking for you when you return, and wary about sucker punches."

"Yes. But I couldn't let them take you."

They moved on. Beyond the village there was a field of wild flowers. Tumble paused to gaze at them admiringly. "They're so beautiful. I always like them."

"And Trevor taught you to appreciate beauty."

"Yes."

"Tumble, what would you do if you had all power in the world and could do anything at all?"

"Oh, I have thought about that! I'd help all the villagers in need, except the bullies, and make nice paths lined with flowering trees, and I'd try to perk up Bleak Mountain."

"Bleak Mountain!"

"I think it's called that because the Sorceress may be unhappy and doesn't take much care of it. But maybe if it had some nice trees and rivers and butterflies, it would perk her up."

"You'd try to make the Sorceress happy?"

"Yes. She's a person, too, even if she is centuries old. If she could look out on a really nice natural scene, she should be happier. Anyone would. Wouldn't you be happy if the castle were nicer?"

She was thoughtful. "Yes, I suppose I would be." Then she came up with another question. "Tumble, if you could have any woman in the world you wanted, whom would you choose?"

He laughed. "That's easy. Just one who honestly loved me. I wouldn't care about her shape or age or anything. All I want is to love and be loved and have a nice family."

"That's so sweet."

He shrugged. "It doesn't matter. No girl ever liked me. None ever will."

"But a smart woman might, if she really got to know you."

"Maybe. But I'm not holding my breath."

"Tumble, *I'm* really getting to like you. I may be only a doll, but I think you're a very nice man, and I'd truly like to make it with you before we reach the castle."

"Make what with me?"

She smiled. "I love your naïveté, too. I'm talking about making love. Sex. I'd like to seduce you, at least once. I promise you rapture such as you have never known or even imagined."

"But if you seduce me, I won't want to turn you over to the Sorceress. I wouldn't be able to make myself do the right thing. I'm weak, but at least I know my weakness."

"Your weakness becomes you, Tumble."

He shook his head. "I don't understand that. I only know I mustn't do it with you. It would—it would violate my honor."

"That's true. You would be no better in that respect than your grandfather Trevor was. He was a good man, but he couldn't resist that particular temptation. But Tumble, maybe I'm worth it. You could keep me the way

Trevor did, and park me in a box between times. I'd be a whole lot of fun."

He was sorely tempted again, but knew it wouldn't be right. "I have to do the right thing. That is to return you to the Sorceress."

She made as if to turn down her halter. "Don't you like me?"

"I like you too much, Pip. I know you're only a doll, but you're really pretty and you seem like such a nice person. But I have to do what I have to do."

"You are so steadfast," she said sadly.

"What would *you* want, if you could have anything?"

"Me? I'm only a doll. It's not my place to want anything."

"But if you could?"

She glanced sidelong at him. "What do you think I would want?"

"To be alive and free, not needing to cater to any man anymore."

"But Tumble, I *like* catering to men. It's my prime entertainment." She paused, considering. "Still, it's a fair question and deserves a fair answer. I think I'd like to be valued for more than just one thing, my evocative and obliging body. To—well, as you said, to truly love and be loved. And have a loving family. I've never had that."

"I wish I could give you that."

She squeezed his hand tenderly. "I wish you could, too. You're the first person who ever asked me about my preferences."

The path became steep. Tumble was panting by the time they reached the front portcullis of the castle. "I guess this is good-bye," he said.

"Not yet. This time I'll do the seductive kiss."

"But—"

She cut him off with the kiss. His whole body reacted with the power of it. His arms clasped her involuntarily and his desire seemed overwhelming.

But he fought it off. "I wish—oh how I wish!" he gasped. "But I mustn't. I promised to return you, and I must not break my word."

She frowned, her anger flaring. "You're a fool."

"Yeah," he agreed miserably.

"Then put me down on the floor inside the castle and let go."

He stepped through the gate, holding her. "I hope the Sorceress gives you freedom at last, so you can be happy." His eyes were burning with tears. "I love you, Pip. Even when you're mad at me." Then with a superhuman effort he put her down and let go. He felt as if his universe were imploding.

But the doll did not reappear. Epiphany continued to stand there, untouched.

He blinked, trying to clear his vision, but the doll was not there. "I don't understand."

"Tumble, it is time for you to know the rest of it," Epiphany said. "The trial is over. You have succeeded in doing your duty. I am more than satisfied."

"Why haven't you changed?"

"Tumble, you said you love me. Would you still love me if I were more than a magic doll?"

The truth was easy. "Yes!"

"Considerably more?"

"Yes. But—"

"I *am* more. I am the Sorceress."

He was amazed. "You? But—"

"I assumed the doll form so I could anonymously get to know different men. Between-times, while the doll slept, I handled my regular business, alone. I like you, Tumble. Like you a lot. I believe I will marry you."

"But I'm not handsome, strong, smart, or rich! I haven't even finished cleaning out the attic."

"I can grant you all these things, in abundance." She smiled briefly. "I'll even help you with the attic. But here's the point: What I can't magically give a man is integrity. You are the first in a century to actually turn in the living doll." She stepped up to him, taking him by the shoulders, gazing into his eyes. "I know I can trust you, Tumble. You will do the right thing regardless of temptations or threats. That's what truly counts."

"But—"

"Tumble, it's been a long dry spell. I have decades of passion backed up. I never got enough from the doll, though I relished what I did get. I simply had to find the right man. You are that man. Please, come to my bedroom. I promise to do the right thing by you, after. I will always look exactly as I do now, unless you come to prefer a change, and will always do my best to make you happy. I have potency spells galore if you ever need them. Your mother will be pleased to see you gainfully married. We'll tour the world. We'll help all your villagers. We'll have children, a loving family. We'll make Bleak Mountain beautiful. Anything you want, as I know you won't abuse it. But right now I just have to make love to you. It's all right, now that you know me and we have a relationship. I'm on the verge of loving you, in my fashion, and that is an extremely rare and wonderful thing for me." She brought her lovely face closer. "Please."

He could not get a handle on his feelings. "But—"

She frowned prettily. "Unless you have a thing against older women?"

"No! I don't care how old you are. I love you! It's just so much, so sudden. You were just a doll in the attic. Now you're—"

"A woman almost in love."

"Mother would be wary of my taking up with a—a strange woman."

Her pupils came to resemble the fiery mouths of two volcanoes. "Not half as wary as she would be of an angry Sorceress."

He was alarmed, knowing her power. "Please don't hurt my mother!"

She was instantly contrite. The pupils became two placid love pools. "I wouldn't think of it, dear. I'm just saying that I'm sure she will be reasonable."

"I—I can't tell you no. But I don't know what to do. I have no experience. I'd be clumsy. I don't want to—to turn you off."

"Fortunately I have experience also, in quantity. I will guide you." She took a breath. "Tumble, I have proposed marriage to you. Do you accept?"

What could he do? He was overflowing with desire for her, and sex was only part of it. "Yes. If it's the right thing."

She smiled. "It's the right thing, Tumble, and it's only the beginning." Then she kissed him, and won him, completely.

THE WHITE KNIGHT
Aric Sundquist

Solomon found the knife in the attic. At first he thought it was a carved wooden stick, but when he gripped the handles and gave a little tug, it separated in half like a katana sword. The writing on the handle looked Japanese, with an intricate dragon etched into the blade. Instantly he knew this wasn't a normal knife. This knife was used to hunt dragons. This knife was feared.

He closed the chest and jumped onto a rickety chair just as a wave of molten lava jettisoned past him and slammed against the cavern wall. He had to be careful opening up treasure chests out in the open. He might not make it out alive next time. That last blast was too close for comfort.

He hopped to the couch, being careful not to touch the attic floor, and then climbed down the ladder and stood in the kitchen again.

The blade shone like polished glass in the sunlight.

"What do you have there?" his grandma asked. "Looks like a bread knife."

"It has a dragon on it," he said.

"A dragon you say? I think your grandfather must have gotten that in the war. It's very old."

She knelt down and tested the sharpness of the blade with her fingertip. "I don't think you could cut through warm butter with that edge. You can keep it, Sol, but only if your dad says it's okay."

"It's okay!" Solomon pleaded.

"But we have to ask your dad first, remember?"

"Okay."

His grandma kissed his forehead.

Solomon thundered back up the attic steps with his new weapon tucked in his belt, and this time he met Talking Cat, who was nailed to a tree. The cat had patchy brown fur and a top hat and liked to practice voodoo and other strange magic. They were treasure hunting rivals.

"What did you find in that volcano?" the cat asked.

"I found a magic blade," Solomon declared.

"Really? Does it dance in the air and attack on its own?

"No."

"Oh. What does it do then?"

"It's the sharpest blade ever created."

"So you found the legendary Vorpal blade that beheaded the Jabberwocky?"

"Yes." Solomon didn't know what a Jabberwocky was, but it sounded weird, and fierce.

"That's amazing! So what name are you going by these days?"

"I am called the White Knight," Solomon said. "I fight for the good guys."

"Well, my friend, looks like you're going to need the help of a powerful wizard. A war is coming."

"I will think about it. Why are you nailed to that tree, Talking Cat?"

"Oh, that. Well, the natives caught me, you see. They don't like renegade toys looting treasure from their island. And they don't like little boys, either, so I would be careful if I were you."

Solomon glanced around the vast jungle. The foliage began growing deeper and everywhere the sounds of exotic birds mingled with tribal drum beats.

"Please help me," the cat said. "My stuffing is leaking out. Do you have a needle and thread?"

"Are you going to behave *if* I help you?"

"Yes, I promise."

Solomon crept up to the cat and tried to push the stuffing back inside the holes, but to no avail. "I don't have needle and thread, but I know someone who can help. We just have to watch out for the cannibals and make it to the raft."

"Then we better get moving. Free me and I will fight by your side with my fire magic."

Solomon unsheathed his blade and pried out the nails. Talking Cat fell to the ground and then stood on wobbly feet and scooped up his cotton entrails.

Then the cannibal toys attacked.

Solomon jumped into action. He struck down the foes with deadly accuracy. Hobby horse didn't have a hobby anymore. Jack-in-the-box didn't have jack anymore. Fabric and plastic limbs littered the ground.

Talking Cat kept his word and fought by the White Knight's side. The cat chanted and held out his paws and magic flames erupted, scorching the jungle landscape, laying waste to all the attackers hiding in the trees.

They fought as a fearsome duo, past the valley of cannibals toys, and finally made it to the raft.

Talking Cat fell to the ground, near death.

"I am on my last breath," the cat confided. "I have lost too much of my stuffing."

"But it's just a little farther to safety," Solomon said. "You can make it."

"You were always my favorite adversary. Now we are friends and I will die a true hero's death. For that I am thankful. You should use your new blade. One strike will end my suffering."

Solomon looked down at the blade. "It's only for fighting bad toys" he said, "not good toys who pretend to be bad sometimes."

"A weapon like that isn't always for fighting evil. Sometimes you need to ease the suffering of good toys, too. It's because they are hurting inside and it's better if they don't hurt anymore."

"But I'll miss you."

"And I will miss you, too, my friend. But it must be done. Sorry I stole all your jewels and pushed you off that flying carpet last summer. There are no hard feelings, right?"

"No hard feelings."

"Take care."

Solomon took a deep breath and slipped the blade into the heart of Talking Cat. He held his friend as the toy went limp and became just an old toy again.

Solomon mourned the loss of his friend. And then he heard real crying downstairs.

He crept halfway down the attic steps and saw his grandmother washing dishes and wiping away tears. She cried a lot lately. He wished there was something he could do to help her. He didn't like to see her sad.

Solomon crept back up the steps. Talking Cat was now shambling around a box of Christmas lights, pretending to be a zombie. "She wants to be with him again," the cat moaned in zombie talk. "She is hurt and lonely and only you can ease her suffering." The cat motioned to the blade.

Solomon took the zombie cat up in his hands and grabbed the string on his back and stretched it out all the way. The motor sputtered to life and MEOWED in a long metallic cat voice, and then Solomon spun him in the air and threw him hard across the room.

"Don't ever say that again!" Solomon shouted. "I'm going to imprison you like a mummy and you won't be able to talk for a thousand years! And I'll put a curse on you, too, so you can't ever leave!"

"But I am already cursed," Talking Cat said from the corner. "You know that."

"Then you'll have two curses."

"Want to know where that knife really came from? I traded it with a merchant in Kyoto, Japan, for two Hershey bars. It was a Christmas present for your grandmother because she loved baking so much."

"I don't care," Solomon said. "You're becoming bad again and I need to put you away. Nailing you down didn't work, so I think I need to bury you deep in the ground somewhere."

"I just had a thought!" Talking Cat said. "There's a sharpening stone in here somewhere. Don't you want your blade to be sharp?"

Talking Cat did have a point, Solomon realized. If his blade was the legendary Vorpal blade used to slay this vile Jabber-thingy, and if he was indeed the White Knight of legend, then his weapon needed to have the sharpest edge in the world.

"Okay," Solomon said. "But no tricks. Help me find the stone and then it's off to the mummy crypts for you."

Talking Cat began shuffling toward the boxes.

"Not like that," Solomon said. "You're a mummy now, remember?"

"Sorry." Talking Cat held out his hands and walked stiff like a mummy. "Like this?"

"Yes."

"You know what?" Talking Cat said as they began rummaging though the boxes, "I know a lot about curses. I was in Haiti for three years, you know."

"I know. But tell me again."

Talking Cat smiled wickedly, and then he began telling Solomon about real curses.

THE DOLL TREE

Amelia Mangan

All the signs are there. Just where everyone told you they'd be. Lining the cracked and broken road, lopsided in the black and crumbling earth: "THIS WAY TO THE DOLL TREE". The letters are childlike blocks, the arrow beneath them a shaky, trembling squiggle. Maybe the sign's writer was starting to have doubts.

Nothing grows here. On either side of the road, crops lie wilted, exhausted, lank as a dead girl's hair. Shiny-eyed crows feast on shreds of purple gore, scraped from hot black tarmac. Thin, pale grass twitches in the hot and unrefreshing breeze, throwing skinny shadow at the feet of peeled-paint fenceposts. Rusting chainlink sways in the wind.

It sees you before you see it. The Tree. Looming over the barren soil from the top of its high hill, lord of this dead land. The size of the thing, the size. Immeasurable strength, unfathomable age. Its thick tangle of roots, sunk deep into the hill's flesh, endless whorls and loops and spirals. Its skinny, scabby limbs burst through the sides and roof and windows of the House, the House that contains it, the House it wears like a corpse wears the suit it was buried in. The House was grand once. Big, impressive. Nowhere near as impressive as the Tree.

Nobody knows which came first: the Tree, or the House. Did the Tree grow up through the House, displacing, assimilating, infecting its brick and mortar, crawling up through its drain pipes, out through its fine brass fixtures, snaking through bedrooms and bathrooms and, finally, the attic, before smashing through its roof, stretching up and up and up, arms high and wide enough to span the empty sky? Or was the Tree here, first and last and always, and the House an organism that grew up around it, a parasite of glass and wallpaper, chandeliers and wooden beams?

It doesn't matter. The House is here, and the Tree is inside it, eating its heart forever.

Climb the hill, spiky grass lashing your legs, dry dirt slumping beneath your feet; push gently on the once-red door. It will open, and the House will admit you.

All the floors have fallen away. Up above and all around you, the skeletons of rooms lie bare and stripped. Here, the remains of a bedroom, now no more than rough wood floorboards and a naked brass bedstead, tarnished swamp-green from rain. There, a bathroom: fixtures ripped from the walls, shattered tiles like broken teeth, thick wet mildew seeping down from the edge of its open facade and poised to spread.

And in the middle of it all, the very soul and spine of the House and its decay: the Tree's trunk. Thick and black and forever. Wooden night.

The spiral staircase wraps around the tree, poison ivy around a forgotten temple's column. No one knows who put it there. You'd prefer not to climb it, but it's the only way. The only way to get to the attic.

You place one timid foot upon the step. The metal is heavy with rust, buckshot with holes, but it holds steady, surprisingly steady. You hold the banister; its cold burns your palm but you hang on, and climb the stairs, one at a time, slow and cautious at first, then faster, more determined, knowing it would now be pointless to go back down.

Your head brushes flat wood. Your flesh rises in tiny bumps, reaching up. The Tree's trunk vanishes into darkness above you, a darkness even greater and heavier than its own. You take a breath, take another. You press close to the Tree. You breathe it in, its sap: molasses-thick, sweet and metal, melted candyfloss and swallowed blood.

You move up, stretch out an arm, feel around with splayed fingers. Hit floorboards. You've found it. You've found the attic.

And you haul yourself up, wrenching your shoulder, twisting around the trunk, until you sit on the edge of the ragged hole surrounding it. Your breath is a cloud. Films of dust cling to your eyeballs; you tear up, blink, stare with eyes as wide as you can make them.

The branches stretch from wall to wall, up and out through the broken roof, the splintered windows.

And every one of them yields the same bounty, the same fruit: dolls.

Dangling from every single branch, hanging from every clawed black finger, every spindled limb: dolls. China dolls and plastic dolls, girl dolls and boy dolls, porcelain and wax, big and small, dressed and naked. All of them dirty, all of them old. A thousand half-lidded glass eyes watch you in the kaleidoscope light; thousands upon thousands of stiff little bodies sway in the stifling wind. Some hang by the neck.

The floor is littered with dolls, the ones that have fallen from the Tree. The ones that were ripe. You pick one up, a chubby, unsmiling pixie; it has a cord dangling down from its back. You hold it taut between thumb and forefinger; it is damp, mildly viscous. You let it go. "Ma-Ma," says the doll, its voice deep and grinding, an old-man death-rattle. You put it down. Quickly.

You walk across the floor, trying not to let your feet touch anything, any doll, navigating winding paths around them until you make it to the nearest wall. One arm of the Tree has punched through here; you move closer, curl a hand around its curiously smooth bark, and lean closer, peering outside.

Down below, a long way down below, behind the House, long and neatly-hoed rows of soil stretch on and out into the far blue distance. Tiny white shoots poke up through the dirt. And though it is impossible to tell, impossible to ever know, what strange seed feeds this dark and quiet earth, one thing is obvious even to you, even from your vantage point high above and close to Heaven: those shoots are not shoots at all, but the fingers of dolls. Hundreds and thousands—uncountable millions—of dolls. Growing in the earth. Growing their tiny doll fingers.

Some of those fingers have prints.

A breeze, cooler than before, waltzes through the attic, strokes your shoulder blades. You shiver. It's still summer now, still hot, dry, infertile summer, but soon the summer will end, and fall will take its place. Soon, the harvest will be in.

A LITTLE TERROR
Phil Hickes

Small hands flash like blades in the half-light of the attic. To and fro, this way and that, they prise legs, pop arms, gouge eyes and yank heads. Movement is economical and precise. The right hand teases glistening, sticky tears from a tube of glue. The left brandishes scissors like cutlasses. Together, they're an industrious blur, knotting string and sticking tape, destroying and creating with equal vigor.

Tools are selected with the same care a surgeon chooses scalpels. There's a tiny hammer, the type a cobbler might use. A pair of rubber-gripped pliers. A screwdriver. A sharp craft knife. Each of them has their part to play. And when the hands are done, the tools are gently replaced in the exact same spot from whence they were plucked.

It is a great work.

A herculean labor.

A symphony long in composition.

Outside, the day has long since snuffed out its candle. In the attic, a solitary bulb flickers feebly, its life slowly ebbing away as it dangles from its black wire noose.

A small figure stands.

Those clever, agile hands take a moment's rest on skinny hips.

Then the figure turns and is gone, thoughts of creation replaced by thoughts of cookies.

* * * * *

Left behind, in the corner of the attic, slumps an abomination. An antichrist of symmetry. Already forgotten by its fickle creator, it lays where it has taken crooked shape, a gargoyle without a steeple. One huge, muscled arm props it up. Another, slim and feminine, points up at the ceiling, frozen in a plea for mercy to an indifferent deity. A third, some kind of woolly tentacle, flops flaccidly to one side.

Stretched out in front are its legs. Or they could be more arms. Even the creator wasn't entirely sure. One limb is metallic and mechanical, the other soft, squishy and covered in lime green fur. They're joined to a jigsaw puzzle torso, an ugly contradiction of plastic, rubber and metal.

Atop its catastrophic geometry, the bitter cherry on a moldy cake, sits a ghoulish head made from robot, doll and teddy bear. A couple of mismatched glass eyes, sourced from other toy-box unfortunates, have been added for effect. The final flourish is the strawberry grin of Mr. Potato Head—an irony of expression that makes mockery of the creature's twisted physiognomy.

It's a thing best suited to the shadows.

For that's where monsters live.

And if left to its own devices, that's where it would stay, an afternoon's entertainment immortalized in deformity. But as the night wears on, dark clouds roll across the heavens and blot out the stars. The air crackles with static electricity. The inhabitants of the house moan softly in their sleep, the atmospheric alchemy creeping into their dreams. A low rumble of thunder sounds in the distance. The horizon flickers like a strobe. A dog whimpers and huddles beneath a kitchen table, tail tucked meekly between furry legs. A storm is working itself up into a fury.

Slowly, sinisterly, it comes closer, a destructive leviathan determined to live its short life to the full. Above the attic, a swirling maelstrom of dark clouds gathers, glaring down malevolently at the fragile building below. A blue-white flash of electricity is spat out and fizzles down the spine of the house. It races up wires and down cables, frantically searching for mischief. A spark flies onto the malformed figure. The fuses blow with a bang. Everybody in the house awakens.

Everybody.

And everything.

* * * * *

At the back of the attic, beneath a cobweb awning, tucked away in the corner where the draughts whisper cold tales, there is movement.

Being, arguably, the most intelligent, it's Cindy the Doll who becomes aware first. Looking down at her new, surgically enhanced frame, she lets out an anguished wail. Downstairs, Cody the terrier pricks up his ears and whines in sympathy.

The screaming encourages Bobby the Teddy Bear's slow stirring, and he awakes to find that his brain is now a co-operative. He feels confused, and then annoyed— curious feelings for a creature that has only ever known loving cuddles.

Lastly, RX82, Killer Robot, activates. Its sensors struggle to assimilate the flood of data coursing through its electronic synapses, and it quickly finds itself faced with a conundrum: there are intruders in its circuits; they have to be terminated; but to do so means terminating itself; and that contradicts its survival programming.

It's a tricky one.

A cold fury has replaced Cindy's hysteria. She wants answers. And payback.

"What's happened to me?" she cries. "Who...what am I? Did you do this?"

"No."

"*Negative.*"

Reply Bobby Bear and RX82.

"Who are you anyway? Why are you in my head? Why is part of me green?" cries Bobby Bear. "Is this your idea of a joke?"

"Certainly not!"

"*Negative.*"

Reply Cindy and RX82.

Meanwhile, the mechanized part of the triumvirate has come to a decision.

"*Doll and Bear to be assimilated,*" it says. "*Prepare to launch counter-strike. Locating targets...*"

"What does that mean?" says Bobby Bear. If he'd had any paws left he might have scratched his head.

"It means, stupid, that we're not going to take this lying down," says Cindy coldly.

She clenches her new muscular hand into a fist.

* * * * *

Eddie Van Twaalfhoven lies in bed listening to the storm recede into the distance. Phew, that was a big one. For a moment he thought the house was going to fall down. He's not scared though. Having just turned nine, he's a big boy now and not afraid of anything. Though at that precise moment, he hears a scratching noise coming from up above.

From the attic.

Despite his fearlessness, he clutches the sheets a little tighter and pulls them to his chin. He knows, as every young child does, that nothing wicked can penetrate the magic bedclothes. Just so long as everything's covered. Leave a stray hand or foot outside its protective barrier though, and you're asking for trouble. Wide-eyed he stares at the ceiling as the scratching comes again, this time a little further along. His lampshade shakes a fraction as a faint thud sounds. A pattern begins to form.

Scratch—thud.

Scratch—thud.

Scratch—thud

It sounds as if something is alive up there. He wonders what it could be. A bird? Maybe a bat? That would be cool. Oh no. Surely Cody hasn't got up there? Did he forget to push the stairs back up? That wouldn't be cool, because it would mean he's in even more trouble. And that's the last thing he wants after the day's events.

It had started with a loud, high-pitched scream, as his sister, Nancy, found the remains of her mutilated dolls and cuddly toys. Instinctively, Eddie had protested his innocence. But as the resident inventor in the house, with a huge canon of work to his credit, he was never going to get away with it. Plan B was to point out that he'd sacrificed one of his own toys, too—a treasured killer robot from Mars.

But that didn't help either.

Punishment had been swift and terrible: exiled to his bedroom without milk and cookies. Now, as he hears his stomach rumble, he thinks of sneaking down to the kitchen and raiding the biscuit jar. Thankfully, the scratching sounds have stopped now. He risks flopping a hot arm outside the coverlet.

Nothing grabs it.

It's safe to come out.

He plans his mission. In his mind he sees himself silently making his way downstairs—the Cookie Ninja. He's just fighting off the evil forces of Nancy when sleep reaches up and drags him back down into its murky depths.

* * * * *

"Ok, what now?" says Bobby Bear, a little breathlessly.

Progress has been slow, their new anatomy proving impervious to any kind of fluid motion. But like reluctant colleagues at an office team-building day, they work together and manage to produce an acceptable, if ungainly, movement. Now they pause at the trapdoor. Its four sides are illuminated by thin slivers of light from below. It looks like the door to heaven.

"Now we get the fuck down from here," says Cindy, her remaining eye staring wildly.

"Yes, I know that," says Bobby Bear, "but how?"

"How the hell should I know?" says Cindy. She moves to slap him with her one of her new limbs, but then remembers that she'd only be slapping herself. Traces of vanity remain, and although she's only been left with an arm, an eye, a slice of cheek and half a jawbone, part of her has a vague memory of once being beautiful. Even now, she wants to look her best. Besides, her arm is now his arm, too. It's all very confusing.

"Wait a minute," says Bobby Bear, "it's...um...I'm...I mean, *we're* onto something."

Cindy and Bobby feel their new robot circuits rapidly processing data. It's the feeling you get when the dentist pushes a whirring drill into your molars.

"Targets located," says RX82. *"Prepare to initiate termination."*

* * * * *

Eric Van Twaalfhoven is seriously pissed off. It's been a hard weekend. Of course it's nice having the kids. He had to fight hard enough to make his bitch of a wife—ex-wife—let him see them. But if he's honest, part of him is glad he's not doing this full-time. He works hard all week at the office, and come the weekend, all he fancies doing is sinking a few beers with the guys and lazing around the house watching the golf. But he's hardly had a moment to relax. Nancy's at that age when she needs constant entertaining, which usually involves having to take her to watch some shitty film about teenage vampires with floppy hair. Two hours of that shit. At least Eddie can keep himself entertained, making all those weird models. Yeah, until he had to go and cut up his sister's dolls. He felt bad sending the kid to bed, but you've got to teach them to respect other people's belongings. And now, just as he was finally catching up on some sleep, the damn fuse-box blows and he's stubbing his toes in the dark trying to get the power back on before the freezer defrosts and he's left with a week's supply of soggy pizzas.

As he's coming back up the stairs he hears a thumping noise coming from the attic. What the fuck? Through the doorway, he can see his bed. It beckons, a warm seductress willing him to lay his weary head on two large, soft, white breasts. But something tells him to have a quick look at whatever's making the strange noise. Like it or not, he's got responsibilities. And if that storm has knocked out something else electrical, well, that's how fires start. Sighing, he pulls down the steps and flicks on the light. As his head appears through the trapdoor, the first thing he sees is one of Eddie's fucked up projects. Some kind of robot-doll-Muppet thing. It stares at him with five lopsided eyes.

He smirks.

It's kinda creepy.

Then it moves.

By the time he's registered that the fucking thing's alive, a red laser beam has shot out from its chest and burnt out both his retinas. Now his face looks like a snowman's, with two pieces of charcoal for eyes.

* * * * *

Nancy Van Twaalfoven is woken by a bump in the night. Not again. She's only just dozed off after the thunder and lightning woke her. But this sounds like something *inside* the house. Muscles tensed, she waits in the dark, her mind already racing away to the dark corners of the imagination where the serial killers and evil clowns live. It takes a while for the rational part of her mind to catch up and usher its irrational sibling back into the 'Reasonable Explanations for Nocturnal Noise' department. So now she thinks:

Cody the terrier on a midnight ramble.

A falling golf club in the cupboard.

A horrible little turd of a brother with a weak bladder.

All of these possible explanations are now given preference. Robert Pattison pouts disinterestedly from her bedroom wall. As her eyelids start to droop, the sound of a tiny voice outside her door brings the dissipating terror rushing back to boiling point.

"Nannnnncy."

The voice is Britney Spears using Stephen Hawking's voice-box. It's weirdly familiar. Her eyes widen and she feels her coiled intestines shift like nervous snakes. She props herself up on one elbow, eyes squinting in the gloom.

"Who's there?" she asks, following it with a hopeful, "Dad?'

"Nancy, come on we want to play!" says the voice again, only this time it sounds like Yogi Bear after a tracheotomy. Under the door she sees a shadow. It lurks, waiting for a response.

"Don't make us come in and get you," says the voice a final time. Hawkings, Spears and Yogi Bear are now all speaking at once.

And then Nancy feels a red mist rise, scattering her fear to the corners of the room. That little turd! Scaring her half-to-death in the middle of the night with his stupid pranks. He just doesn't know when to stop! She tears back her bedclothes and jumps to her feet, her pretty mouth twisted into a determined grimace.

Yanking open the door, she glares out, expecting to see the idiotic grin and tousled bed-hair of a nine year old turd. Instead, the corridor is silent and empty. She feels a soft scratch on her ankle. As she looks down, she sees a set of fleshy bagpipes, lidless eyes of all different sizes staring up at her. She recognizes parts of her doll and teddy bear in there, too, and even amidst her terror, there's a stab of righteous indignation. The thing starts to pulsate and throb, a collapsed lung desperate for air. As it slithers towards her bare feet, she's too scared to move. So when a plastic arm stretches out clutching a craft knife, it doesn't have far to reach to slice neatly through her Achilles tendon.

* * * * *

Nancy's screaming again.

Eddie's eyes open for the second time that night. He lies still, as dark outlines of bedroom furniture emerge shyly from the blackness. He wonders what her problem is now. Probably thinks she's seen a mouse. But even as he thinks it, he knows that it's not true. This was a real scream.

Blood-curdling.

Something is wrong.

He waits for the sound of his father's bedroom door opening, the sound of strength, reassurance and decisiveness. But it's not forthcoming. And now he's faced with a dilemma no nine-year old should ever have to ponder.

What to do?

To his credit, he immediately swings his legs up and out of their protective cotton cocoon, feeling the cold night air immediately rush in to prey on his warmth. Padding softly across the varnished floorboards, a boy-panther, he reaches the door and pauses, before bending down and placing his ear against the keyhole. Eyes wide, he strains to listen.

Silence at first.

Then fragments of whispers. A quiet cacophony of malicious, manufactured voices.

"...commence final stage..."

"...can see him, he's behind the..."

"...cut it there, where it's soft..."

"...why are you telling..."

"...hush, stupid, he's listening..."

Eddie stands, quickly looking around the bedroom for a makeshift weapon. There are things out there. And they're coming to get him. The survival instinct kicks in, that hardwired defense mechanism that lays dormant within all of us, waiting to be summoned in times of need. A miniature golf club is seized, the one that he uses with his father. It's cut the air to pieces on many occasions. Now he needs it to connect with something more substantial.

Back to the wall, he pulls it up behind his head, a perfect swing that would have drawn a gasp of admiration from Van Twaalfhoven senior, had he still possessed eyes to see. Then he waits, legs trembling.

Light floods in.

Retinas shrink.

As the door slowly swings open, the young boy learns that fear simply doesn't know when to stop. Once it has you on the rack, it can always push you a little further, no matter how much the bones crack and the joints pop and the skin tear.

The strange voices come again, gargling in unison.

"Where have you been hiding, we've been looking all over for you!"

Eddie screams.

He'd be mortified to know that he sounds just like his sister.

* * * * *

After a furious night's work, many arguments, and a lot of blood, the Van Twaalfhoven family are reunited. What's left of them is reminiscent of something cast on an amateur potter's wheel, only clay has been replaced by flesh. A cadaverous termite mound now sits on the landing of the house, chunks of flesh wrapped up in glistening gray tentacles of intestine. Like a pizza that's been overturned in its box, the individual parts have become indistinguishable from the mass, though one can occasionally recognize the black olive of an eyeball, or a salami slice of kidney.

It's a collage of corpses.

The family get-together from Hell.

Cody the terrier is the only one left untouched. Being of a cowardly nature, he's spent the night shuddering in his basket, as agonized cries and unearthly voices echoed through the house. Only now does he dare show his furry face, hunger finally conquering his cowardice. He mounts the stairs nervously, confused by the aromatic union of father, son and daughter. A hopeful wag of the tail. A whine as he sees the scarlet sculpture ahead of him. The bottom of it drips rhythmically, a melting popsicle of blood and gore.

Even his simple doggy brain can recognize an obscenity, and for a moment he experiences an agonizing sense of loss.

But being a dog, it's only a moment.

He's still hungry after all.

And, well, beggars can't be choosers.

* * * * *

Cindy, Bobby Bear and RX82 are at something of a crossroads in their short lives.

"*Mission accomplished,*" says RX82. For a moment his metallic tones are infused with sadness.

"Yeah, awesome work team, that showed them," says Cindy emptily.

"That was fun!" says the irrepressibly optimistic Bobby. But everyone knows he's just putting on a brave face.

And then it's quiet, none of them knowing quite what to say or do.

"So what now?" says Cindy, "I still look like a dog's dinner."

"Funny you should say that," says Bobby.

"*Organic life-form detected,*" says RX82, weakly.

One toy would be exciting enough for Cody the terrier. But now he sees huge pile of them, all conveniently lumped together for his enjoyment. Having just enjoyed the finest feast of his life, he licks his bloody chops and switches to PLAY mode, which is one of only four modes that he possesses, the others being EAT, SHIT and HIDE. He used to have HUMP, too, but that disappeared on the day a veterinary took his balls.

Cody gallops towards them, wagging his tail furiously like a demented orchestra conductor.

RX82 is spent, a night of slaughter having exhausted its batteries. It just doesn't have the will to fight.

Bobby Bear is delighted to be given one last chance to play. Mutilating people always felt a bit odd anyway.

Cindy is relieved. For a girl that's been used to the finer things in life, being a bit player in a mutant cephalopod has been unbearable. As Cody's right fang sinks into her mascara-lined eye, she embraces oblivion.

This whole thing has been a nightmare from start to finish.

GIVE IT A NAME

Gary McMahon

It is time.

You have waited years for this moment, trying to forget, to put it out of your head, but it has finally arrived. Even your wife, before she lost her mind and was put inside an institution, could not convince you to face the reality of what is meant to happen. You preferred to wait, and to tell yourself that you would solve the puzzle before the allotted time ran out.

The clock strikes midnight and you cannot help but smile: so clichéd, so like every scary story you have ever read. A chill breeze enters the room, wafting across your face, and all of a sudden you smell the fetid odor of wet soil.

He is here; he is already somewhere inside the house.

You could just sit and wait, but that would be too passive. You feel the need to act, to take the battle to him, so you pick up the gun from the table at your side, get up from out of the chair, and walk slowly across the room.

The lights are out. It is dark inside the house. He probably feels more at home in darkness, but for some reason you do not want to turn on the lights. Is it because you can't face how he looks, not for a second time? You'd rather encounter his goblin-like features in the gloom?

You stand by the door and listen. The house is quiet. There are no sounds of footsteps in the hall; there is no creaking of timber as somebody slowly climbs the stairs.

Gently, you open the door and step out into the entrance hall. The house is massive. You made a lot of money—it was always part of the deal: fame, riches, success beyond your wildest imaginings—and have been able to afford all the good things in life.

You walk softly across the varnished wooden floor, trying not to make a sound. You have lived here for eight years, so you know every loose board, each separate groan the house might make as you move through it. He doesn't know any of this—he is an intruder, an alien in your midst. Your familiarity with the house gives you an edge, or so you tell yourself, keeping up the pretence that you have a chance of changing things.

Shadows skim across the floor and huddle like frightened animals at the bases of the walls. You ignore them. They are nothing, just tricks of the night. The real trickster—the one you have waited the best part of a decade to meet again—is waiting for you somewhere within the house, grinning with that hideous oversized mouth.

You check the living room, but he isn't in there. The grandfather clock stands like a blind sentry, the leather armchair is a fat dwarf waiting to pounce. The fire grate is an open mouth.

You turn around and walk towards the library. The door is open, and when you peer inside, half expecting to find him there, poring over the old books in your collection, all you see is the dark interior of the shelf-lined room. The books you paid so much for, the signed and limited editions, the first editions and forgotten volumes, are all worthless to you now. The only thing that is worth anything is upstairs in an attic bedroom, behind a bolted door and with an armed guard—an ex mercenary and former SAS man known only as Mr. Timbre.

The kitchen is empty of life, too. Just pots and pans and cabinets packed with food. The walk-in freezer is locked, as always, and he wouldn't be in there anyway.

He hates the cold.

He likes the heat, just like the devil he is.

Finally you return to the hallway and begin to climb the stairs, one hand on the banister, the other clutching the pistol. You aim the barrel forward, in case he decides to jump out on you, like a jack-in-the-box. But he doesn't do that; it isn't his way. He prefers a more subtle approach.

At the top of the stairs you stand and stare along the landing. All the doors are closed. At the end of the landing, around the corner and up another short flight of wooden stairs, is your son's attic room. Toby is asleep. It is his tenth birthday, and you let him stay up late to watch a

DVD. He fell asleep before the end, and you carried him up the stairs and to his room, with Mr. Timbre bringing up the rear just in case you-know-who (or, more to the point, you-don't-know-who) decided to make an appearance earlier than promised.

But he wouldn't have done that, either. He is nothing if not a man of his word. A man…is that really what he is? Right now, at the dead of night in a darkened house, you think not. Everything he promised you came true: all the riches, the magazine covers and television shows, the films and the awards, and all the money that fell into your open hands, making you a multi-millionaire almost overnight. No mortal man could deliver on such a deal.

You check each room as you move along the landing, just in case. It feels as if you are simply delaying the inevitable. You know where he is, you have always known. He is exactly where he said he would be: in your son's room, waiting for you to make your own entrance. But this is all part of the game, a way of deceiving yourself and pretending that the legends were all lies, stories told to scare children into behaving themselves.

Fairy stories.

He isn't in either of the two guest rooms. Nor is he in your room, the master bedroom, with its huge bed and thick carpets. The showroom; the best room in the house. No, he isn't in there. You know he isn't, yet still you are compelled to look, to continue with this absurd delaying tactic.

Finally you reach the turning at the end of the landing. You stop, take a deep breath, and tighten your grip on the gun. Your palms are sweaty; the gun feels like it might fall from your hand. You close your eyes and remember…you remember how it all started…

…as a struggling artist in a cramped council flat in east Leeds, waiting for opportunity to come and find you. You would have done anything to make it to the big time: sold your soul, traded your flesh, even given away your firstborn son, who at that point was not even a flicker in your imagination. You never wanted kids. You didn't think it would matter…

And that was when he came. It is always when he comes. Just as that thought enters a person's head, put there by the fairy tales of their youth, he stirs in his nest of baby bones and rolls onto the blood-sodden ground of his underground cavern, hearing the clarion call of yet another desperate soul, a man or a woman so in love with the thought of a short cut to success that they would give anything to achieve status and respect without having to work hard, to sweat blood and tears, without having to earn it.

In the story the code is cracked, his name is always learned or overheard at the last minute, just in time to save the day. But in reality, things are not so simple. He either doesn't have a name or he has so many that it is impossible to pin one down and present it to him when he comes a-calling.

Mr. Timbre has travelled the world trying to learn the name he goes by, but always he returned without a clue. An old man in Tibet was meant to know the secret, but when Mr. Timbre reached the village where the man was supposed to live, all he found was fifty dead bodies and a bunch of burned-out huts, the embers still smoking. Then again, in India, it was claimed that a woman was the keeper of his name, that she had it tattooed on the inside of her mouth. All Mr. Timbre found was an old painting of a woman with her jaws held open by metal rods, and a question mark carved into the flesh of her tongue.

There is an obscure tribe in a remote part of the Andes whose members worship him, venerating him as a deity: a harsh God who steals children, who consumes their flesh and picks clean their bones with his long, thin talons.

He does not have a name. Or perhaps he has too many.

You turn the bend in the hallway and see Mr. Timbre on the floor at the foot of the attic stairs, a pool of blood forming a perfect crimson nova around his head. You mourn him only briefly—he was a good friend, a dogged worker for the cause, but in the end he was unable to help. You bend down, touch a hand to his forehead, and close

GIVE IT A NAME

your eyes, saying a prayer to a God in which you have never believed.

Then, accepting the truth of the situation at last, you stand and approach the stairs that lead up to your son's bedroom door.

At the top of the stairs the handle is twisted; the big heavy-duty Yale lock has been broken in half. The door is ajar. You reach out and push it open, not stepping inside, not yet; just waiting on the threshold, waiting to be invited in.

"Enter." His voice is the same as before: high-pitched, childlike, a mockery of humanity.

You step up into the attic room and close the door behind you, never looking anywhere but straight ahead. Not at the flickering television set in the corner, the shelves and cupboards, the cartoon posters on the walls. Staring only at him, directly into his terrible watery eyes...

He looks identical to the last time you met, ten short years ago. He has not aged a bit—but, strange-looking as he is, you probably would not have noticed any effects of ageing on his distorted features. He is short, perhaps four feet tall and as thin as a bunch of sticks. His hands are long, large: they are the hands of a giant grafted onto the arms of a dwarf. He is wearing red felt ankle-length trousers, a short green waistcoat with nothing underneath. His ribs are so visible that the grey skin covering them looks like parchment paper. You are sure that you can see the motion of his heart beating, the slow flow of blood through his monstrous veins.

"It's nice to see you again." His lips are like skinned sausages, framing a mouth that takes up most of the lower part of his perfectly round face. His nose consists of two black holes located an inch above the top lip. His eyes are the size and shape of saucers, with lots of white pupil and tiny red irises.

You are unable to speak.

"What's wrong? Cat got your tongue?" He is holding your sleeping son, with one of his painfully thin arms wrapped around the boy's neck, like some kind of variation on the sleeper hold used by nightclub bouncers and old-school wrestlers. He tightens his grip. Your son sleeps on, drugged by either narcotics or magic.

"Let him go." Your voice, when it comes, is pathetic; quiet as a whisper.

He laughs, his shoulders shrugging gently. "Don't be so damned silly. I've come to collect on your part of the bargain."

"Please…"

He laughs again. "That's exactly what you said when you asked me for fame and wealth and all the treasures of the modern world. 'Please', you said. 'Let me have it all.' I told you the cost back then, and it's the same now. I'm taking your first born son. In ten years, a man gets hungry."

His tiny feet wiggle at the end of his thin legs. He is wearing purple velvet shoes, with little bells on the pointed toes. But the bells are silent; they make no music. Now is not the time for music of any kind.

"Take anything else—take me. Just…just not him. Not my boy." You fall down onto your knees, holding out the gun. The barrel is shaking.

"Bullets don't work on the likes of me. Just ask your dead friend out there. He tried that one, too, until I slit his throat with my fingernails." He laughs again; the sound is empty, mocking, and it makes you feel physically ill.

"You have one chance now. Remember? Can you remember that part of the bargain, the single get-out clause? You have one chance to save your boy, and to save yourself." He pauses, strokes your son's damp blonde head with those long, long fingers. The nails are like knives, and stained red with Mr. Timbre's blood. "Just tell me my name and I'll leave. It's as simple as that."

You begin to cry, but soundlessly, not wanting to give him the satisfaction of hearing you sob. "But it isn't easy. Not at all. I've searched everywhere, spoken to everyone who might have the slightest clue, but I've never found a thing. Nobody knows who you are. You have no name."

"Oh," he says, opening that enormous mouth to show oversized wet, pink gums without any teeth. Gums meant for sucking, not biting. "Oh, but I do have a name. If you think about it, my name is obvious."

You taste the word before you say it, and it makes you retch.

"Rumplestiltskin."

This time his laughter is uproarious, as if what you have said is the funniest thing he has heard in several lifetimes, the greatest joke of all time. "Oh, don't be so fucking stupid," he says, between bouts of manic laughter. "I expected so much more from you."

"I…I don't know your name." Everything you say is obsolete. Nothing sounds right.

He gets up off the bed, dragging your son along the floor by the neck. Still Toby does not move; he is out of it, deep under the influence of this twisted little man, this goblin from the darkest recesses of the human mind.

"Please, just let him go."

He shakes his head. His pulsing eyes are filled with sorrow. "I don't like doing this, but it's necessary. Such is my lot in this life; to take away the ones you people love most and eat them like a good steak, sucking off the succulent skin and devouring the tender sweetmeats beneath." He licks his lips; his thick tongue, when it unfurls, is at least a foot long and covered in livid spots. Contrary to his self-serving soliloquy, he looks as though he enjoys this very much. "All you have to do to save them is tell me my name. It's easy if you put your mind to it, so damned obvious. But nobody ever guesses right—they're all too caught up in that stupid fairy tale, the one read to you by your stupid parents when you're lying gurgling in your cribs."

His eyes are shining. They are aflame. He shakes his head, and then continues with his rhapsody:

"But let me tell you something, my friend. Those fairy tales are all lies; they are perfect little deceits, designed to cover up our real intent. That's precisely what gives them their power." He walks slowly to the small dormer window, hauling your son onto his broad, square shoulders before delivering the kicker, the punch line. "That's what gives me my power…"

You do not want him to leave, not now, not like this, with Toby hanging from his shoulders like a potato sack. "Do one thing, then...before you leave." You point the gun at him, your finger tightening on the useless trigger. "Tell me your name."

He pauses with one leg raised and his foot resting on the narrow window sill. The window is open. A chill breeze ruffles his sparse hair. "I won't do that," he says in his curiously singsong voice. "But I will tell you this:

"I am the oil in the water, the canker in the rose, the tiny spot of blood at the center of the egg yolk. Mine is the first and the last story ever told. I walk through walls and I dance around the fire like nobody's watching. My blood runs with the molten lava of youth but I have been around for centuries, playing my games and telling my stories. I am famine and pestilence, I am illness without cure. My name is written on the underside of the rocks at the bottom of the ocean; it is whispered by eagles in flight and carved into the inner walls of volcanoes. I am chaos, I am destiny, and I am the one who always wins the fight. I am you, I am him, and I am her.

"I am everyone."

Then, in a flurry of movement, the imp is gone, leaping over the window sill as if the burden he carries is as light as a doll. His footsteps clatter across the roof tiles, quick and light.

The window rattles in its frame, the breeze flutters the edges of the posters on the walls, curling them, and the sweat dries like paint on your suddenly cold skin. Much too late, you pull the trigger but the gun does not fire. It was never going to fire, not while he was around, exerting his influence and playing out his grim little games until the world ends...

You drop the gun and crawl over to your son's bed, then climb up onto the mattress and curl up into a ball on top of the bedclothes. You can smell his skin. You pull his stuffed toys close, cuddling them as if by doing so might change this thing that has happened. Among them is a toy you have never seen before, a final insult left behind by that monster. It looks just like him: thin arms, big hands, round grinning face…

You close your eyes and see liquid fire surging behind the lids: the burning walls of a volcano, the inside of the throat of a dragon, the molten belly at the core of the planet earth.

Lava. Magma. The blazing fires of eternity.

Written there in jagged lines of light, burned deeply into the shifting stone ceilings of underground caverns, you finally see his name, and the irony is so damned perfect that it breaks your heart in two. The truth was there all along, right behind your eyes, but you didn't have the sense to notice. His name has never changed. It has always been the same, eternal and immortal, just like him…a name that will never, ever die.

"Tell me my name," you whisper though the tears.

"My name," you answer, smiling and shivering and trying to imitate his voice.

"My name is…Forever."

DISCARDED
Nancy Rosenberg England

Blake was tired of waiting in the attic. He was just tired period. It felt like it had been a very long time, but he wasn't sure. He also wasn't sure what he was waiting for. He wasn't hungry. Or thirsty. Maybe he ate and drank before he came to the attic? He couldn't remember before the attic, though. His head hurt.

A squirrel ran across the floor in front of him, right over his foot! Blake froze.

The twenty or so forgotten dolls surrounding him stared blankly in various directions. Some stared at the wooden dollhouse, the one that was never painted. Some stared at the shoe boxes filled with ancient cassette tapes— R.E.M., Tears for Fears, Van Halen. Some simply stared into the attic itself, a slanted space no more than four feet high at its highest point. A small window allowed filtered light and Blake saw that the sun was going away.

One doll was a Chinese girl named Ling with a lovely porcelain face, thick dusty black hair (real?), and a long white nightgown. The lace at the end of its nightgown was yellowed but still beautiful. Its expression was solemn. Most of the dolls wore solemn expressions.

The Barbie doll didn't look like the one in *Toy Story 3*. Its blonde hair was chopped off and parts of it were missing, revealing small holes in its head where hair used to sprout. What was left was streaked green, maybe from a magic marker. It wore a pair of neon pink stiletto heels and nothing else. The little yellow dress by the boxes of puzzles might look nice on it, but Blake was too far away.

Baby Boy, the favorite, was propped up against a curly auburn-haired Cabbage Patch Kid named Nathaniel Xander that was lying flat on its stomach. Baby Boy's eyes were so big and blue. Its soft, well-hugged pajamas were tattered and spots of dried applesauce painted its bib. It looked like a real baby and that its owner dearly loved it, maybe even took it on strolls in the turquoise and white

125

bassinet in the corner. And it blinked! At least Blake thought it seemed as if it could blink if someone were to hold it.

The Alice in Wonderland doll looked confused to be in an attic and not a wonderland, but its lips still yet formed a sweet bow. Blake thought it was pretty. Maybe it could be his girlfriend some day! But his head hurt right now. What a pretty blue dress and white apron. Why, it even held a pocket watch! Was it real?

The fancy, boxed Winnie-the-Pooh tea set was out of Blake's reach. The illustrations on the tea set's box were marvelous, though. Kanga and Roo with raised teacups; Piglet and Pooh Bear giggling, eating tiny cakes; Owl looking down on them, stern yet pleased. Alice might like to have a tea party with him, Blake thought. He would serve whatever people served at tea parties.

Blake stared at Alice, at all of them, and they stared back.

After a while, they bred long shadows that looked real. The lace at the end of Ling's nightgown was a cobweb, stretching across a chunk of the attic. Barbie's stilettos and breasts were sharp weapons. Baby Boy was nothing special, just a lump. Nathaniel Xander was a corpse floating in a river. And the Alice doll cast the tall, intimidating shadow of an angry adult; its pocket watch was a large rock. The rest of the dolls were a jumble. Blake couldn't find his shadow.

As much as he liked Alice, he didn't want to be among the dolls. He didn't want to be in the attic with these strange shadows that turned nice into scary. The shadows stared at him and he stared back.

Then the sun was gone completely and it was dark. The attic smelled like wood and paint. It was warm and quiet. The neighborhood in which the house in which the attic existed was warm and quiet, too. Residents used sprinklers in the summer so that their lawns remained a vibrant green and paid sincere-faced teenagers to shovel snow from their long driveways in the winter. Leaf blowers cast off unwanted leaves in the fall and in the spring…well, the spring was something to see. Spring rain stirred crocuses, daffodils, and tulips from the formerly dead land into landscaped perfection. A heavy gate was intended to prevent persons of possibly unsavory inclinations from gaining access to the comfortable community.

The barking dog that startled Blake sounded far away. Had Blake ever met that dog? He bet it was a nice dog, one that licked children's faces and wagged its tail very fast. Its barking grew louder, closer.

Banging. Louder banging and now shouting. There was a struggle with the lock on the entrance to the attic, a small wooden flap on the floor. It finally popped open and in the sudden light the head of a gray-haired man with a mustache appeared. He looked like Santa, or maybe a relative of Santa's.

"Santa?" Blake asked.

"He's here! I've got him! I've got him!" The man pulled himself through the flap and crawled over next to Blake. He put an arm around him. "It's okay now, Blake." He called toward the voices under the floor: "There's some dried blood on his head, but he's conscious and looks good!"

"They shoved me up here and I hit my head." Blake touched his head where it hurt and also his ankle that felt funny. "They were mad." Tears fell on his soft cheeks upon remembering that he'd made them mad again somehow.

"Well, you're okay now and nobody here is mad at you." The police officer smiled and Blake smiled, but his big blue eyes didn't; they were blank. The police officer noticed this and asked, "Are these your dolls?"

"No, they're Mama's. Can Alice come with me? For a tea party."

"Of course, buddy, anything you want. You don't belong here with these old toys. You're not a toy."

GOOGLY

Jeremy C. Shipp

We eat chocolate cake for breakfast, and when my mom asks me how it is, I give her a big smile that fills up half my face. The truth is though, I'm sick to my stomach, and every bite makes me feel that much worse. I keep imagining my parents kneeling beside my shriveled corpse, slicing off strips of flesh from my bones. This probably won't happen, but when it comes to matters of life and death, probablies don't make me feel any better.

After I finish my cake, my mom stacks up all the plates and says, "Are you excited about today?"

"Yeah," I say. There's so little truth to my answer that it's probably a lie.

"You're going to do fine." She squeezes my arm, hard, as if to say, "You'd better do fine."

My father stands. "It's time."

I glance over to say goodbye to my mom, but she's already in the kitchen.

"Stand up," my father says.

I obey.

My father gazes down at me with sad-looking eyes that remind me of a puppy. "You look frightened."

"I'm not," I say.

"There are worse things than facing your own potential death."

"I know."

At this point, my dad wraps his enormous arms around me, and I can't help but imagine him snapping my spine in two. But he doesn't, of course. He lifts me and carries me up the stairs. I'm fully capable of walking to the attic on my own, but this is tradition.

Once we reach our destination, my father throws me across the room, and I land with a hard thud on the wooden floor. Then he reaches into his jacket pocket and pulls out a box wrapped in ugly yellow paper. He tosses the gift at my feet.

"Happy birthday, Simon," he says, and turns toward the door.

"Dad. Wait. Can't you tell me anything? What am I supposed to be doing in here?"

Without another word, my dad leaves the room and locks the door behind him.

I glance around, rubbing my arm. There isn't much to see. A few cardboard boxes, a dangling light bulb, a circular window about the size of a dartboard. There are bars on the window, just in case I get any funny ideas. Really the only interesting thing in here is the pile of bones in the corner that once belonged to my sister. Now they don't belong to anybody, I guess.

For some reason, I'm a little surprised to find my sister's remains up here. I'd always assumed that my parents had at least buried her in the yard. But why would they go to that kind of trouble for someone like her? She failed her test.

I try my hardest to remember her name. I can't.

With nothing better to do, I rip up the ugly yellow paper and open my birthday present. I don't expect anything but a wad of cash, because that's what they give me every year. But inside the box, I find a familiar face. Well, if a smooth black stone with one googly eye can be considered a face.

"Mr. Googly," I say, smiling.

So I can instantly recall this rock's name, but I can't for the life of me remember the name of my own sister? At this thought, I feel something close to embarrassment.

I dump the rock out of the box into my hand. He feels heavier than I remember.

When I was really young, I would take Mr. Googly everywhere. The park, the grocery store. I would even take him to school with me. Sometimes, I would reach my hand into my pocket and rub my thumb against his puffy plastic eye. At night, I would place him under my pillow.

I don't remember where Mr. Googly came from, and I don't quite remember when he disappeared. I thought he was lost for good.

"Do you know what I'm supposed to be doing in here?" I say.

The stone stares at me, silent.

I pocket him, and walk around the room like the ball in a pinball machine. I know I'm in this attic to prove myself. But what does that mean exactly? If I don't figure out the answer to that question, I'll end up dying of thirst, and then my parents will eat away at my flesh until I look like my sister.

My stomach gurgles. Sweat trickles from my armpits. I reach into my pocket and caress Mr. Googly.

After a while, I get bored with walking around the room, so I decide to put together my sister's bones like a jigsaw puzzle. I'm no good at anatomy, so I'm sure some of the bones are upside down or in the wrong spot entirely. It doesn't matter.

While I'm working on the puzzle, I try to conjure up an image of my sister in my mind. It takes me a couple minutes to come up with anything. But finally, I remember her long brown hair. As soon as this detail comes to me, my right cheek begins to tingle.

Then another memory surfaces. I remember sitting on my bed, asking when my sister would come back. My mother slapped me, hard, on my right cheek. She said, "You have no sister."

I remember asking her the same question again and again. She always gave me the same answer, in the same way.

At the bottom of the bone pile, I find my sister's doll, like a prize at the bottom of a cereal box. The doll has one blue eye and one black eye.

"Do you know what I'm supposed to be doing in here?" I say.

The doll stares at me, silent.

After I finish putting together my sister, I search through the cardboard boxes that are lined up against one wall. There isn't much to see. VHS tapes, old magazines, a crumpled up fedora. I'd like to wear the hat, but after giving it a sniff, I decide to return it in the box.

Really, the only interesting thing I find in the boxes is a rat skeleton.

For no good reason, I decide to replace my sister's skull with the tiny rat's skull. After I finish my creation, I take a few steps back and admire my work. I laugh.

As the day goes on, I get hungrier and thirstier. But there's nothing to eat. Nothing to drink. When the sun starts going down, I pull the cord hanging from the ceiling, but the bulb is burned out.

Soon, I'm lying in the darkness next to my sister. I can just barely make out her little rat head. Her doll sits inside her ribs like a prisoner, and I hold Mr. Googly in my hand.

In my dream that night, I'm sitting on an enormous bed, wearing ugly yellow pajamas. The air here smells like dust. If I look carefully, I can see the dust particles swarming before my eyes like fireflies. I want to get out of bed, but I can hear Something crawling on the wooden floor, circling the bed. The Something never stops moving, not even for a second.

I know I should peek over the edge of the bed, but I don't want to see the Something's misshapen face. I don't want to look into its beady black eyes.

My stomach gurgles. Sweat trickles from my armpits. I reach under my pillow for Mr. Googly, but he isn't there.

Finally, I can't hear anything anymore, and I know that the Something is gone.

But instead of feeling relieved, I feel more alone than ever.

The next morning, I search the attic for food and water. Of course, there's none of that here. Well, I could eat spiders or drink my own urine, but I guess I'm not that desperate yet.

Like yesterday, I pace the room, trying to figure out what the heck I'm supposed to be doing in here. I'm thirsty as hell, and every once in a while I glace at the mason jar in the corner that I peed into. Nope. Still not that desperate.

Maybe I'm supposed to prove myself by showing off my fighting skills? As far as I can tell, there's no enemy in here for me to defeat, but why should that stop me? I grab one of my sister's femurs, and wield it like a sword. I attack the imaginary warriors around me as if my life depends on it. And maybe it does. I show off my best skills, but the attic door doesn't open.

After a while, I collapse next to my sister, breathing hard, smothered with sweat.

Maybe I'm supposed to prove myself by showing off my intelligence? Lying on the floor, I recite the Pythagorean theorem, like the Scarecrow in *The Wizard of Oz*. Then I regurgitate as many dates and events from World War II as I can. After that, I move on to literature, and I summarize *A Tale of Two Cities*. The attic door still doesn't open.

I turn to my side and look at my sister's little rat face. "I'm going to die in here, aren't here?"

She stares at me with hollow eyes, silent.

For a moment, I picture myself banging on the door, begging my parents to let me out. As if that would have any effect on them. The thought makes me laugh.

I stand and pace the room again. While I'm walking, I hold Mr. Googly in my right hand. I massage his eye. I try to think, but my mind feels like a stinky old fedora that won't do anyone any good.

Eventually, while I'm squeezing Mr. Googly, I get the sensation that someone's holding my hand. I can feel this Someone's fingers interlaced with my own. It doesn't feel like I'm holding a rock at all.

I look at Mr. Googly, and he's still just an ordinary black stone.

"Hmm," I say.

I can't remember anyone ever holding my hand, but for some reason, the sensation feels familiar. My parents would never have touched me like this. Maybe my sister?

Finally, the memory crawls out of its hiding place.

When I was a little kid, I used to play a game with Mr. Googly where I would lie down in my bed, naked, and I would touch him against different parts of my body. When

I held him in my hand, I would pretend that someone was holding my hand. When I touched him to my ear, I would pretend that someone was whispering to me.

But right now, it doesn't feel like I'm pretending. While I'm squeezing Mr. Googly, it really feels like someone is holding my hand. Maybe I'm hallucinating.

Curiosity gets the better of me, so I strip naked and lie down. I use my T-shirt as a pillow. Hopefully there aren't any hidden cameras in here. I don't want my parents seeing this. Then again, I could be dead soon, so what does it really matter?

Just like when I was a kid, I start off by balancing Mr. Googly on my forehead. I close my eyes. I take a few deep breaths. I concentrate on the feeling of the cold stone pressing against my skin.

Minutes pass, and I feel stupider and stupider, lying there naked on the floor with a rock on my head.

But then, something happens. It's only a faint sensation at first, but in time the feeling grows in pressure. I feel as if someone's leaning over me, kissing my forehead. Warmth spreads throughout my body like a drop of bright red food coloring in a cup of water.

I open my eyes. Of course, there's no one there.

Next, I place Mr. Googly on my lips. I don't actually remember putting the rock on my lips when I was a kid, but I want to see what happens.

Time passes, and I feel someone kissing me on the lips, gently. My chest aches. I want to reach out and wrap my arms around the Someone above me.

I consider positioning Mr. Googly between my legs, but there really could be a hidden camera in here, so I decide against that. Instead, I lie on my side, and rest the stone against my ear.

Soon, I hear a woman whispering. She gets louder and louder, and eventually I can make out what she's saying.

"I love you, Harold."

Who the fuck is Harold?

Then I hear a little boy. He says, "Daddy, Daddy! Pick me up!"

There are other voices, too. Men, women, children. I even hear a cat purring at one point. I hear the name Harold over and over again, so it seems to me that all of the voices are speaking to this one guy in particular. Who all these people are, I have no clue.

The voices don't say anything especially mind-blowing or interesting. What the voices have in common is that they're all speaking in soft tones. After a while, I can't even hear the words anymore. The voices become like music, like a lullaby.

My breathing slows. My muscles relax. This is the closest I've ever come to sleeping without actually being asleep. It's as if I'm soaking in a hot bath after spending hours in the rain without an umbrella.

In this peaceful state, a memory bursts into my head. I remember lying next to my sister in our bedroom. With her eyes closed, she held her doll against her ear. She smiled in a way that didn't look at all menacing.

I open my eyes. After removing Mr. Googly from my ear, I crawl over to my sister. I remove the doll from inside her ribs. The doll has one blue eye and one black eye.

With my bare hands, I rip apart the doll's face and remove the black eye. Just as I suspected, the eye is actually a smooth black stone, the same shape as Mr. Googly.

So my sister grew up with a special rock just like I did. We used these toys to comfort ourselves as children, to make life easier. To pretend that we were human.

When my dad gave me Mr. Googly as a birthday present yesterday, I assumed that it was a sort of warning. I thought he was saying, "You can die a child up here with your little toy, or you can grow up and live." But Mr. Googly is more than a simple warning, isn't he?

Unless I'm hallucinating all of this, Mr. Googly is imbued with some sort of positive energy. He's filled with voices and caresses and kisses. Are these memories? Harold's memories? If these are memories, then why are all the memories so soft and sweet? Why isn't there any pain?

Maybe this rock is only imbued with those moments of warmth in Harold's life that managed to touch his soul.

Maybe this rock is Harold's soul.

I stare at Mr. Googly as he rests on the palm of my hand.

"You're why I'm here, aren't you?" I say.

He looks up at me with a puffy plastic eye, silent.

To be honest, there's still a big part of me that wants to play with Mr. Googly. But if I'm ever going to grow up, I have to leave that part of me behind.

When my sister was trapped in the attic years ago, maybe she figured all this out. Maybe she just decided that she'd rather die than grow up. She was a fool.

"I don't want him anymore," I say, and I throw Mr. Googly at the floor.

I sit and wait for the attic door to open.

It doesn't.

I wait for what seems like an eternity, and I feel myself growing weaker and weaker.

Eventually, I crawl over to Mr. Googly and study him carefully. I turn him over in my hands. I poke his eye. Mr. Googly is the key to all this, but I'm not sure what more I need to do or say.

I hold the rock close to my face and say, "Help me."

I know it's stupid to ask a soul for help. Mr. Googly, or Harold, or whatever his name is, doesn't care a thing about me. He's not my friend. He's living in his own little world, away from pain, away from me and my kind. Why should he get so much while I get so little?

Without thinking, I stick Harold in my mouth and I break him to pieces with my pointed teeth. My father once told me that souls are an acquired taste. To me, Harold tastes like dust. As I swallow him, part of me wishes that I could absorb the soft voices and caresses and kisses. But of course, all of this passes right through me. All that remains in my chest is a dull ache of pleasure, knowing that I've destroyed something precious.

A moment later, I'm writhing in agony on the wooden floor as my new horns burst through my scalp. I reach out to my sister, hoping to hold her boney hand, but she's too far away. Soon, my parents are standing above me with smiles that fill up half their faces, and I know I've passed the test. And I feel more alone than ever.

RUBIK'S CUBE
Melanie Mascio

I wake up sometime in the middle of the afternoon. It's Monday. I look up at the ceiling and think: how interesting, that it's there; that it's white; that it's above me, not too close and not too far; that it hasn't fallen down in the night. I feel compelled to write about the ceiling. First I have to get out of bed. This is not always an easy task. Definitely not on a Monday.

The room that awaits me—my office—is not much bigger than a hummer limo, but square, and in it lies an infinite range of possibilities—books, crayons, pictures, toys, a Polaroid camera, and a computer loaded with mindsweeper, solitaire, and scrabble—none of which are on my list of things to do. I think about the room—once I finish contemplating the ceiling—and how I don't want to go in there. Not because it lacks charisma or because it's messy, but because in it awaits that one necessary and certain possibility, which *is* my list of things to do today. I need to draft the last chapter of my dissertation: "The Formal Considerations of Popular Sculpture."

"Mrrrrrow."

I roll over onto my stomach. I feel a tingle in my groin as my stiffened penis rubs against the sheets. I have to pee. I know I'm not lazy. I'm simply tiring...

"Mrrrrrow...Mrrrrrow."

My focus shifts entirely to these meows, which aren't actually meows, but loud, penetrating moans, revealing a not-so-hidden, not-so-deep meaning about the cat's current state of being, which mimics my rumbling stomach.

"Mrrrrrrrrrrooooooooow."

The moans compel me to roll around a bit, eventually, albeit haphazardly and inadvertently, resulting in my stepping off the bed. I'm vertical.

"Two, four, six, eight, ten...thirty-one." It can't be an odd number. Step back, step forward, thirty-two. Thirty-two steps from the bedroom to the workspace. Too quick

139

and too smooth, even with all the pit stops: the bathroom, the kitchen, and then the bathroom again. Soon enough, I'm face to face with that definite and certain possibility lying on my desk, which takes up half of the room and, on the bright side, is both literally and figuratively facing the great outdoors.

It doesn't take long for me to begin to wonder at the glorious courtyard before me. How amazing is that ivy, strategically attaching itself to my apartment walls, forming a pattern reminiscent of my very face. And look at those massive sunflowers, giant banana-hue lollipops of sweet joy, leaning slightly toward my window, inviting me to come outside and sniff their fragrant petals. *Love to, not today.*

The sun grows brighter in an instant. Its rays point toward my desk, giving the papers a fluorescent glow. I sit down and turn my thoughts away from the courtyard and onto the overwhelmingly abundant and sloppy pieces of paper on my desk, at my feet, and under my buttocks. I know I'm forgetting something incredibly important.

The Smurf puppet!

The Smurf puppet is missing and I must find it immediately.

The sun's rays illuminate my entire desk and all the books and all the papers. Even my computer is glowing. In an effort to block the sun, I pull back the floral curtain barely hanging on the window in front of my desk. I will find that puppet! I check behind and overtop the bookshelves, littered with books and torn aesthetics journals, rustling crinkly papers from left to right and onto the floor. I move the shelves outward, crawling behind them. *Achou.* The dust is killing me. *Achou. Achou. Achou.* Always in threes. No, it was four.

"Mrrrrrrooooooooow."

I eagerly push aside some books and papers that have fallen behind the shelves. An ancient art history notebook pops up among them. I cast it onto my desk. *Air Guitar* by Dave Hickey turns up beneath it. I cast it onto my desk. I come across some missing papers for chapter 1. I cast them onto my desk. I crumple seven old to-do lists and thrust them behind me. And then I push aside mounds of dust-bunnies that lie underneath.

"Mrrrrrrrrroooooooow."

"Shut up, Kitty!"

I stare down at the empty floor, and then quickly brush the dust off my fingers. I step out from behind the shelves, and sit down on my swivel chair. Defeated, I swivel. I swivel in the other direction. Gawking once again in amazement at the courtyard, concerned about the whereabouts of the puppet, I begin, slowly and strategically, to tug at the tiny hairs on my forearm.

I begin to type. *"Alas, the missing papers have been recovered. The implications of this are infinite…"*

I'm in a groove. I forget about the puppet for a brief and calming moment. Then without effort comes the realization that the puppet most certainly sleeps inside my very desk, in a drawer, way in the back, amidst all the junk, in a box of fellow treasures recently rescued from my parents' attic. I impatiently open the drawer and begin to toss out everything that isn't that Smurf puppet: seven rogue staples, three old business cards, a Polaroid camera, and five instant photos fall to the floor. After what seems like a fruitless, endless, cyclic task of finding, tossing, counting, finding, counting, and tossing, I forget what I'm searching for, as I find myself hysterically spinning the tiny squares on my Rubik's Cube.

I don't find the puppet. It doesn't matter.

Not a moment wasted. With every second, bands of tiny squares are forced in and out of the sockets with the help of my aggressive hands—my fingers growing callous from all the winding, the palm of my hands already irritated from the earlier tugging. *I should find some W-D40 and oil that cube.*

The sun disappears. There's nothing to see without the sun's rays. My office light has been out for three days. I don't care. I could feel my way through the different colors just by way of them slipping in and out of the sockets. I turn on some calming music: Brad Meldeau's piano version of Radiohead's "Exit Music for a Film" overflows from my I-book speakers. The cube is fighting me. I can't get that second red square where I want it without throwing off either one white, one yellow, or one orange square. Frustrated, I lay my head on my desk and fall asleep. Every single square, save for the red one, exactly where I want it.

The morning sun awakens me. I've chewed off three of my ten fingernails in my frustrated sleep. There's no more music; there is only the sound of some birds playing outside my window. Kitty is staring at me intently from upon the desk. I should get some real *quality* rest before starting the day.

Mrrrroooooooww.

"Dammit, Kitty."

In an attempt to swat Kitty from my desk, I inadvertently shove the cube onto the floor. It's not how I left it. All of the red squares are mixed up in the blue squares and the orange and yellow squares are scattered among them, mingling with white, green, and pale orange ones. Perhaps I dreamt of the near perfect cube? No. I'm certain I dreamt of the bedroom ceiling. Perhaps I shoved the squares out of place in my restless sleep? No. I'm certain I only flicked my fingernails onto the floor. Looking down at the pile of fingernails, defeated, once again, and exhausted, I begin to gnaw on what is left of them.

A feeling of rejuvenated skill, coupled with newfound motivation overcomes my state of exasperation. I reach for the cube, which accompanies me to the bathroom, the kitchen, the bathroom again, and then back to my workspace. The squares, clanking in and out of their slots, are cooperating entirely with my agenda. In only a few short hours, all of the colors are matched up precisely the way they should be. How amazing what has just transpired! My joy ultimately lulls me into a deep, satisfying sleep.

I wake up sixteen hours later.

"One, two, three, four, five, six, seven, eight…thirty two" steps from the bathroom, the kitchen, and then to the bathroom, and back to the kitchen, seven steps from the sink to the fridge, eighteen steps to my office, and then… *"What the hell!"*

142

RUBIK'S CUBE

I wipe the guck out of the corners of my eyes, just in case it is obstructing my already faulty vision, and because, upon a single glance over my shoulder and over at my desk, I see the cube is not how I had left it. The perfectly matched colored squares are an ugly mess of mixed up reds, yellows, greens, whites, and blues. I turn toward the bathroom, but then quickly run back to my desk. I sit down on the swivel chair, swivel around three times, no four, and then pick up the cube. I hold it close to my face, feeling my way around the tiny squares and sockets. None of the squares are how I left them. The cube has been tampered with. My entire existence has been blackened with deep-seated anxiety about the state of this Rubik's cube. This anxiety manifests as a sharp chill causing my body to shiver from the bottom up. For a long time, I just sit there, peeling away at my cuticles.

My next impulse: check the windows. There are so many windows in here—three in my office, four in the bedroom, a whopping five in the living room, one in the kitchen, and another in the bathroom. All of them are locked. I scan the room for something more. There's a shoe-sized hatch underneath the floor in my bedroom. Ignoring the fact that it is far too small for anything capable of moving the cube to crawl through, I check the hatch, which has, in fact, been left open overnight. This fact is meaningless, and I know it. *Some crazy glue just in case.* "Stay on the task." I check the front door, the front door, and then the front door. "Two, four, six, eight…"

"Mrrrooooooooooooow."

The phone rings. I'm not answering. What's happening here is far more important than anything anyone could possibly have to say to me—even my mother, or the chair of my dissertation committee, who I've been avoiding for eight, solid months.

"Leo. It's Mom. Where've you been? You missed your sister's birthday. She's a little hurt. Call her. Don't tell her I told you to. And call me when you get this. Hope you're getting a lot of work done. I know you are. Love ya."

I feel sane for a moment. Taking advantage of my moment of sanity, I sit down on my swivel chair and pick up the cube. But not before leading Kitty outside to the courtyard.

Hours pass and I cannot get the cube anywhere near completion. I need a break. I need to go to the bathroom. I need some water. When is the last time I've eaten? Sunday? What day is today? I don't have time for that now. I feel optimistic. My futile, unproductive, poor excuse for a day need not color my entire evening.

I'm wrong. I cube straight through the night. My fingers are numb, and they're already cracked and bleeding from tearing off my fingernails and cuticles. I keep going, cubing and counting and counting and cubing, counting and cubing and cubing and counting. The once stiffly clanking squares have loosened up entirely by morning. The sun shines bright and then disappears once again as night falls.

Two days pass and I have not left the swivel chair. My mouth is dry and bitter, my legs are stiff, and my pants are soaked with urine. None of that matters. The cube is *perfecto*. I reach for the Polaroid camera lying on the floor underneath my desk. A sharp pain shoots downward from my neck to my lower back. I pick up the camera, take a picture of the cube, and sit it beside the actual cube. Satisfied and exhausted, I try to stand, but I fall to the floor.

A few hours later I'm awakened by several more of those loud, penetrating Kitty moans, this time coming from outside my apartment. I look up at the ceiling. So glad it hasn't fallen upon me in the night. I inch my way onto the swivel chair. I look toward the courtyard, which invites me once again to come outside and play. The sun is bright, this time illuminating a concordant row of orange squares. I feel a crust around my right nostril where my nose-ring has gone missing. I lick the blood off my forefinger and pull off some of the crust. The crust reveals itself as dried blood. I recall the dream in which there is a snotty crust along the inside of my nose. In an attempt to clear my runny nose I pulled my nose-ring through the hole and caused a bleeding which had become crusty in the night. I must have slept longer than I thought. Neither the blood nor the sleep matters. I have the completed cube and I have a photograph to prove it.

I feel groggy. A little dizzy. Slightly dazed. Gratified. I move my fingers around my nose to pick out the dried blood. Like a pumice stone on torn feet the blood soothes my callous fingers. I create leftward circles of dried blood with my fingertips. I reverse directions. *Which way now?* I look up at my desk. The picture has been shredded completely. The state of the cube is no longer detectable on the photo paper. I anxiously reach for the cube, my hands shaking with terror. The concordant row of orange squares was an illusory blend of red, orange, and light orange ones. All of the cube's squares have once again been displaced. I grip the cube tightly with my hands, clenching my right fist around it, the tension penetrating my body from this fist up to my head, which causes a sharp stabbing pain inside my cranium.

The windows are closed; the door locked; the hatch sealed; Kitty is outside. I have no hair left on my forearms, no more fingernails or cuticles, I have peed myself several times in the past few days, and I have a bloody crust surrounding my right nostril. I reach for the cube and begin to pull apart each of its tiny squares. In no time the once-Rubik's Cube is a meaningless pile of multi-colored rubbish. I begin shoving the squares into my mouth, one by one, sucking on each of them until it is soft enough to chew—the red ones *seem* to take hours, the orange only minutes. The taste is oddly salty, most likely from my sweaty palms. It is not until I have just about finished chewing the last red square that I realize what happened to the puppet.

I begin to write, safety in the knowledge that both the puppet and the cube, which had once taunted me so, are trapped within the bounds of my belly, mutilated, drenched with partially digested food. They can't hurt me now.

A BRIGHTLY-COLORED BOX FILLED WITH STARS

Dorian Dawes

There is nothing perhaps more unnerving or unsettling than taking a walk in the rain on a busy sidewalk amongst crowds of other people. Drenched despite their black umbrellas, all huddling together, eager to make the next taxi cab or to at least hurry inside out of the cold, it is the one time I have seen where men forget their outward appearances, and let the human masks we wear drop. In the midst of this great gathering of their peers, they are naked and unconcerned for their nakedness, and the horrors of men's souls are laid bare.

I looked into the face of a killer one day, I am certain of it. His jaw was tightly clenched and his eyebrows were furrowed together, and there was an agitated nervousness about his movements and his gait that betrayed him from the rest of us who were hurrying out of the rain. I could see his darkness. His guilt was plastered with the raindrops all over his face. Monsters lie in all men, I suppose.

For whatever absurd reason, be it madness or morbid curiosity, I elected to forego my original errands, and chose to pursue him quietly. Keeping track of him was not difficult; in the midst of the somber procession of soggy black umbrellas, his was a brilliant scarlet that stood apart from the others, a red beacon shining out to me, begging for me to follow. He kept making frequent glances behind him, and for a brief while I was certain he had spotted me following, though he never once made eye-contact. I realized it was nothing but a guilty paranoia dogging his footsteps, threatening him with every gesture. When he turned around, I saw genuine fear in his eyes. He was terrified of being pursued. He was terrified of me.

The terror brimming at the corners of his eyes only seemed to fill me with a mad sort of glee, and it made me reckless, too eager to get close to him. A part of me had the sick desire to be spotted by my prey, just so I could see the revelatory panic upon his face when his worst fears were realized. This was power, I thought, intrigue and adventure, to be the one in pursuit instead of being pursued, a primal instinct that lurks within all men, the hunter and the hunted. It is a game that is as old as the human race, a return to our old selves as animals, and I could only defend my inexcusable, childish behavior with my unsupportable suspicion that this man I followed had somewhere done some wrong, and that it was my duty to expose his misdeeds.

My imagination raced to every possible morbid scenario: of a wife who'd overdone the evening meal for the eighth time in a row, and the need for good nourishment had caused him to snap and stab her repeatedly in the chest with a kitchen knife; or perhaps he was a teacher, and one of his pupils had mouthed off for the final time, and so this man had kept his student after class so as to ensure that he'd never interrupt another soul with his incessant gabble ever again, by hiding the remains of his hacked up body parts in the ventilation for some other poor sap to find. It was also possible that all of these things were quite wrong, and that the reality was more grim and gruesome than anything my mind could come up with. I would only learn by following him to his destination, where surely he was headed to cover up the remains of his crime.

My prey led me away from the main streets and into the darkened labyrinths of our city's back alleys, a swirling, winding infrastructure populated by the sleeping homeless and passed-out drug addicts lying next to abandoned beer bottles and overflowing dumpster-bins. The stench of their filth burned the insides of my nostrils and I knew we were treading into dangerous areas, places of the city where few men dared go for the crime and the corruption, the seething underbelly of the city's underworld, and the further I chased him the darker it became. He was leading me somewhere, and I knew he could tell there was another following him. He'd long since stopped looking over his shoulder.

A BRIGHTLY-COLORED BOX FILLED WITH STARS

After a long while of this constant running and chasing and my heart beating swiftly to the point where it ached inside of my chest, it stopped raining, and he ran into an area where the sun shone into a spot completely unlike the rest of the dark areas in the alleyways behind the derelict buildings. Here there was not only sun but grass and flowers, and little blue-birds nesting inside a well-trimmed tree, and at the end of this well-kept little yard and its pristine-white fence was a small two-story home with white shutters and a door painted red.

I am certain he knew of my presence, and yet still I kept myself hidden in the darkness as he approached the door, closed his umbrella neatly beneath his arm, and knocked three times upon the hard wood. It opened to him almost immediately, as if he'd been expected. He reached into the folds of his jacket and produced a large lollipop, the kind with a rainbow spiral that goes towards a white center and a red ribbon tied around the stick. I watched in morbid fascination as a withered hand, shriveled and claw-like reached from the darkness beyond the door and plucked it from his hands. It then crooked a finger at the man, who followed it into the strange and cheerful home. The door closed behind him all of its own accord, and a sense of dread began to build within me.

Every frightful fairytale ever spoken to us as children began to flit through my imagination, and I was reminded of the cottage from the story of Hansel and Gretel, and of the witch Baba-Yaga of Russian lore. Here was a house so strange and disarming for how peaceful and pleasant it looked, hidden amidst the filth and the darkness of all that was around us. How many years had it been here? I'd stumbled upon a great mystery, and my curiosity, despite my trepidation, would not be sated.

I was about to draw closer to the strange house so that I might peer into the windows and spy upon the meeting, when the voice of a small child caused me to stop before I'd even stepped into the sunlit clearing. "Today is not your day."

Turning around, I came face to face with a dirt-covered boy with tousled blond hair, and in his hands he

149

held a red balloon. His overalls were covered in the grime of the alleyways. He lived here. He looked up at me with a blank, soulless expression and in his eyes I saw a seriousness that demanded I take his words to heart.

"When will it be?" I asked him.

"She only takes one a day," the boy said and walked past me, into the sunlight. "If you want to be granted an audience with *Her* you must come back when you have the thing she wants."

I thought of the present the man had offered to the darkness when he'd neared the door. "The lollipop?"

The boy shrugged. "It is different for every one. Each person's soul is different, the gifts they offer *Her* are also different. Yours will be unique exclusively to you, and when you find it, you will know it is what she wants."

"Who is she?"

The boy laughed and let his balloon forth from his hands; it floated up until it became a red dot against the sky. "She is light and she is darkness. She is a black hole that swallows stars, a distant nebula rising. She is our mother, and the eater of innocence lost."

"Who are you?"

The child again laughed at me but did not answer. He walked to the door and opened it. The blackness ate him up, and again the door closed on its own accord.

As I crept once more back down the alley ways, towards the safety of the public streets, I kept making frequent glances behind me, watching that strange sunlit area shrink further away, until it was entirely obscured by the muck and the grime of the city's hidden darkness. I wondered that I should find it again without my guide. Is it a place that disappears when you look for it, one of those rare things in life that you stumble upon and then it is lost forever, like a strange song on the radio, or a painting that moves you and you can't find the artist? I dreaded it'd be one of those beautiful, unattainable things that simply becomes a memory in the back of your skull, never to resurface, gradually fading until all that you can remember is that at one point there was something wonderful and it made you feel strange and now you are haunted by the memory of something lost that may or may not have ever even existed, a dream that vanishes upon waking.

The insanity of the child's riddle began to replay itself over and over again in my mind, but memory of the event was already growing hazy and the actual words itself were distorting and melding themselves together in my mind so that soon all I could hear inside my head was, "She is our mother. She eats stars." And then I had emerged once more into the sad faces of humanity, every one cast in a pale shade of gray, their faces sunken and their shoulders stooped, tired and on their way to the banks to cash their checks and pay their bills. Only I could walk upright and smile, as I had with me the remnants and the traces of magic and mystery, and I promised I would return to that house and its enchanting light in darkness, even as I took a taxi-cab back to my lonely apartment building. The beauty could not, would not be lost.

There were times when I missed my old home, back before Joann left and took my son from me, and the Judge had ruled that I was not to be granted custody of my only boy. I thought of how I might like to pick him up in my arms when I walked in the front door, and tell him of the strange thing that Daddy had found, of the little boy and his red balloon, and the sad-looking man with his lollipop, all meeting in a clearing of light behind a dark alley, to see the Mother of Stars. Joann wouldn't have liked such a story, as she preferred her calendars and her meetings and things wrapped up in briefcases and corporate conference calls that kept the money flowing. That's why she left and stole our boy, because my delusions and dreams would set him up for heartache, and that without me in his life, he'd be more grounded in reality. Sad, dreary reality. There is no room for a poet in her world.

My son had left his bag of marbles the last time I'd seen him. They're all I had left to look at now. I thought to give them back when he came to visit next Christmas, but that was still eight months away, and so for now I slept with them underneath my pillow every night, and would often count them to make sure they were all there: two cat's eyes, six blackies, one toothpaste, and three oxbloods. I know them all by heart.

That night there was a marble in the bag I did not recognize, a shiny blood-ruby. You could look through it, and see your world painted in scarlet. This was it. This was my key to gaining an audience with the old woman inside the strange house.

The following day I saw a headline in the morning paper, a cop that had gone undercover to investigate a series of disappearances involving several businessmen had likewise vanished supposedly after uncovering a new lead. This did not surprise me, it is after all our city, the place of vanished souls. There's something alive about these streets, like they're a monster unto themselves, eagerly swallowing up anyone who might stumble upon the wrong thing. There was a picture of the cop. It was the man who I'd followed yesterday into the alleys. Any sane or smart man would have left the matter alone after that, but I have been accused of possessing neither sanity nor intelligence and so slipped the foreign blood-colored marble into my pocket and took to the streets once more.

That Sunday morning was remarkably quiet for our city, and I remember distinctly a strange fog accompanying the unusual silence pervading the city's streets. There was not a car nor a soul to be seen, and the fog was so thick it blotted out the landscape for miles. I tried in vain to find the particular alley I'd chased my police officer down, but it seemed like the route itself had vanished.

I had prepared to call it quits and return home to wait for this unnatural fog to lift when I heard the sound of children's voices. Across the street from me they were playing jump-rope, and singing a strange song in time to their little games: *"She is light and she is dark. She is a black hole that swallows stars. She is our mother, the eater of innocence lost. Have something missing returned to you, but be warned there is a cost."*

I watched their faces. They were expressionless and pale. The intonations of their song was not one befitting a children's game. No, it was more apt for a funeral's dirge.

Behind them lay the alleyway, and instead of being the narrow and winding path it'd been when I'd raced down it yesterday, there was only a straight shot forwards. I could see the sun peeking through the fog behind it, and the green grass in the clearing all the way from across the street. The house was making itself known to me. It wanted to be found.

The children stopped singing as I approached them, and instead fixed me with their cold, empty stares. As I passed them and disappeared into the alley, I turned my head back to see they were still watching me, and I am certain they watched until the fog created a wall between us. Like the day before, the weather cleared and I found myself standing in front of the house, with the marble clenched in my sweaty fist. I approached the front door and knocked sharply three times, and tried to still my nervous breathing.

As opposed to the monsters that I'd expected to come to the door there was the little boy from yesterday. His face and clothes were clean, and his hair was trimmed and neat. He looked up at me and then beyond me. I turned around to see that the children playing jump-rope were standing but a few feet away, their eyes boring holes into my back. They'd followed me through the dark, and I hadn't heard their footsteps. I turned back around to face the pale-skinned boy standing in the doorway.

"Normally she doesn't take them in so soon after the other, but for you she is making an exception," he told me, his tone authoritative and haughty, "Do not offend her with your rudeness."

I hadn't even the chance to ask him what I'd done that he'd found so rude when he grabbed me by the hand and pulled me further into the house. I turned around just in time to see all the children standing on the doorstep, just as the door was closing behind me. They were all waving at me and staring with mournful eyes. My guide vanished into the next hallway, and I heard a kind, grandmotherly voice whispering to him.

"Oh, he is here is he? You've done very well. Go play with the others, I'll take care of our guest. I'll be fine, go on, go. No, not today. You've had enough sweets. Now, now, I said no. This one's for my personal collection."

The room was filled with a warm light from an above chandelier, revealing a quaint dining room adjacent to a small kitchen all done in brightly colored tiles of reds and greens and yellows. An old woman wearing a shawl wrapped around her, hobbling on a cane entered the room next to me, and looked up at me over half-moon spectacles with the broadest smile and the kindest eyes, all buried in a face of wrinkles that had seen much laughter. She eagerly approached me and grabbed me by both of my hands, my palms facing up. Her fingers traced the lines in my palms feverously, and then she patted the top of my left hand, and held it in her trembling grip.

"Yes, you are the right one. Someone who is seeking, yes?" she said, her voice on the brim of a tinkling laughter.

"I am seeking…something," I said.

"I just said that, didn't I?" She burst into that set of giggles that had been lingering on the edge of her words and then she turned around to lead me into the kitchen. "But you're not sure of what you are seeking. The answer to a mystery yes, but what are you hoping lies in that answer? Something lost, I should say. We only look for things that are lost, I find. Is chamomile all right?"

"Chamomile?"

"Tea, child! Tea!"

"Yes, that's fine."

"Sit down! Sit down! I'll be with you in a moment." She went rummaging throughout the kitchen, throwing open cabinets, and humming quietly to herself. "And if that something is lost, then it must be something we used to have. Only because it is lost, we cannot remember ever having it. So, the key to finding what you are missing is to remember what it is you are seeking, the thing you no longer have."

Her words confused me, and I wondered how much of this was all part of her performance, her mystique. Everything bore with it the airs and the guise of a practicing fortune-teller, like a gypsy caravan I'd seen as a child, and I'd heard similar jargon. The obvious differences of course laid in the presentation of the mystery, the gypsies were cold and frightening, and this woman burst with maternal love and affection. I felt very much like a small child in her presence, and it would have felt odd to not refer to this woman as a member of my family, Aunt or Grandma seemed more apt titles to her than stranger. What kind of product could she be selling? What service did she seek to provide?

I remembered the poem sung to me by the children. "Innocence is something that I have lost, but I will never have that back."

She emerged into the dining room with a tray full of tea. "Innocence, yes. It is drummed out of us as we grow older, by well-meaning parents and teachers alike, and by the time we enter the real world as adults, we have been sapped dry of it. It is such a difficult thing to preserve. Fleeting and rare."

The old woman began to pour my tea. I took it from her and she beamed at me.

"But," she said, sitting down in a chair across the table, "It need not be lost. It need never be lost. It can be regained. You can have those things back, and can keep them forever, if you'd like."

I did not once take a sip of my tea. "But how?"

She smiled again, and I saw something in the darkness of her eyes that resembled the night sky, and within it many stars. "The key is simply to never grow up."

I was going to remark that by this time for me it was too late, and there was nothing that could be done to save me when I heard a series of voices from outside the window. I looked out to see the series of young, mournful faces looking at me from outside the stained-glass panes. They were singing again, their high-pitched chorus sad and eerie:

"Take heed, young sir, false prophets dwell upon those things straight from hell. You'll want to scream, you'll want to cry, but once she has you, you'll never die."

"Wicked brats! Demon hoodlums!" the woman cried, climbing from her seat and rushing to the window. The children fled the minute she stood.

"Who are they?" I asked her.

"Tormentors of mine, endless thorns in my side," the old woman said and turned around to fix me again with the warmness of her smile. "They're convinced I'm a witch. But don't worry, they cannot harm us in here. And you're wrong, anything that is lost can be found again. Wouldn't you like something you're missing?"

I thought of my son. I thought of Joann.

"I am missing many things," I whispered.

The old woman pointed to a nearby hallway, and a set of stairs illuminated with a faint emerald light. "Go up into my attic. There is something there of mine that will help you. I want you to have it."

Something you have lost…all talk of innocence and adulthood fled my mind as memories of those moments with my former wife flooded back to me. Those happier, poorer times in which money had not been a concern, and there'd only been the promise of new birth. We had our dreams and nothing else, and the stars promised to be our guides, not Wall Street or Stocks or Bonds, but each other and our million hopes. I eagerly rushed to the stairs, thinking that there was a promise to return to those days, to hold her in my arms again, and to have my son hold me as a hero in his eyes. Yes, this was innocence. This was perfection. I'd risk everything for it.

I ignored the many creakings of the steps below me, and the ominous flickering of the light overhead, rushing only upwards into the dark, and to the door to my salvation, the attic. I pushed on it, and emerged into a cobweb-ridden room of dust and decay. Old wood floors greeted me, and I felt for the first time since stepping foot into that cheery house, the monotone bleakness of gray reality. The room was filled with hundreds of dolls, porcelain and plastic alike, each staring at me with a thousand eyes. Some of them were in pieces rolling about on the floor, and some had bits of their faces shattered in after having been violently dropped, and some had no eyes at all.

In the center of the room, where light streamed in through an oval window was a small, brightly-colored box, coated in many years of grime and dust. There was a yellow star on its top, and as I neared it, I saw that it was a lid that could be opened.

Tentatively, I placed my hands on either side of the box and pulled the lid back on its hinges. There was a slight whir as the gears inside began to turn and a tinkling melody could be heard. A music-box, I thought. How is a music-box to help me regain those things I sought?

It was the last thought I would have in my current state, followed by the realization that within that box was a darkness so deep that it appeared to be an endless pit, a stygian void that threatened to swallow me whole. My mouth suddenly sealed shut, and my eyes remained fixed forwards. I saw before me as the room itself seemed to grow and expand beneath my dwindling gaze the faces of one of the many dolls in the room. The eyes were made of glass, though within them was panic and horror, and in its tiny porcelain hand, it held a lollipop with a red ribbon wrapped around its stick. I found that the blood-colored marble I'd brought with me stuck to my hand.

When the music was over, I was innocent, for I became empty.

There is nothing but darkness now. My spirit has joined the children outside, and we are bound here, trapped to this place. Our whispers and songs of warning do no good, and continually there are souls drawn to *Her* presence who join us.

She is our mother, the eater of stars.

THE TEA-SERVING DOLL
Mae Empson

Hikari sailed to the lumber town of Seattle aboard the tea-laden Miike Maru when she was four years old. "This will be a new life," her father said. "Look at the fireworks," her mother added, as they pulled into the harbor. On that day, she imagined that they would always be together, and that she would always look to her parents to guide her steps in this strange new place.

Only ten years later, in 1906, the rhythms of her parent's routines seemed hopelessly old-fashioned to her. They rose early, and insisted that all chores be done long before sundown. "There is no hurry," she argued, "we have electric light at night now." Many of the houses in their wealthy merchant neighborhood in Nihonmachi— Japantown—had recently acquired this luxury.

"Some things should not be done after dark," her mother insisted. Over time, her mother had shared many rules of this kind. Never whistle after dark, or a snake will come. Don't cut your hair after dark, or ghosts will be able to enter your house. Don't try on new shoes and clothes until the morning. Never cut your nails after dark, or you won't be with your parents when they die, and it will happen sooner than it should have. "The night is cruel," her mother warned.

Hikari thought it was ridiculous to be afraid of such things, and indulged in a midnight grooming session— trimming her hair and nails, and trying on new clothes— just to show that she was not afraid.

And so, when her parents died two months later in a boating accident and left her an orphan at fifteen, she had no one but herself to blame.

* * * * *

Her father's business partner took over the tea shop and, with it, Hikari, but he treated her as a servant rather

159

than as a daughter. He made her sleep on a mat in the tea shop at night, rather than take her into his home as a true daughter. She had no other relatives on this side of the ocean to notice or protest.

He sold her family's house, and all their fine things, and kept the money for himself. What he could not sell, he stuffed in a box and stored in the attic above the tea shop.

She watched the attic door, cut into the ceiling of the tea shop, as she worked all day and all night cleaning behind the customers, an endless series of chores that took her far longer than she could recall ever requiring from either of her parents.

She knew that he used a special long pole with a hook at its end to unlock the attic door, which then swung open, releasing a retractable wooden ladder that slid all the way to the floor.

Everything left that could remind her of her parents, that might even still smell of her parents, would be in that box, accessible to her, if she could only get the hooked pole. But, he brought it with him to work in the morning, and took it home with him at night, never letting it out of his sight.

He would forget some time, she kept telling herself, if only she watched and waited. When the opportunity came, she would take it.

* * * * *

At last, one night, he did forget.

She fumbled with the heavy pole and its hook until she found that she could anchor it against her stomach, to help keep it at the right angle to connect the hook with the latch. The door swung down, and the ladder clattered all the way to the floor.

She set the pole down, and climbed up the wooden ladder into the dark space of the attic. She felt along the walls and in the air above her head for some kind of string or switch to trigger a light, but found nothing.

She crawled between the boxes, felt for openings, and slid her hand in trying to determine which might contain her parents' things. She felt papers, fabrics, and something slick and flat that might have been a tintype plate. Everything smelled musty. There were many boxes. Which was the one she wanted?

Cold ceramic, round, like the circle of her fist. A shock of hair. Fabric. A doll? She traced thin arms to a cup. Her mother's doll! Her Chahakobi Ningyo, or tea-serving doll.

Her mother was much too old for conventional dolls, but this was something that had been in her family.

Hikari's mother had told her before she died that it was very precious, and that Hikari should keep it with her always. She said the doll provided greatest comfort with a private cup of koicha—the thickest, strongest tea.

This was the right box. She lifted out the doll and then sifted through the other contents with her blind fingers. She pulled out what felt like photographs and tintypes. He could not sell those, and she wanted pictures of her parents more than anything.

She tucked the doll and pictures into the crook of her arm and climbed back down the ladder into the tea shop. By the light of the shop, she could see the pictures. Her mother and father. The three of them together. Portraits of each of her parents separately. She could hide them under her sleeping mat, and look at them at night when she was most lonely and frightened. It had been worth it to brave the attic.

She lifted the doll to her face and buried her nose in its fabric gown, that hid its clockwork springs. She thought she could catch the faintest hint of her mother's perfume. She cradled it in her arms, grateful that he had not sold it. She supposed it was too well associated with her mother and the tea shop, and would have raised questions about how he was handling their property.

The tea-serving doll had been a clockwork marvel in her mother's family for a century, and was still a conversation piece when her mother had demonstrated its use and spoken with pride about its history at the tea house.

When a tea cup was placed on its tray, the weight of a full cup triggered a mechanism so that it would roll forward towards the person being served, nodding its head in an oddly human rhythm. When the recipient picked up the tea cup, the doll stopped. If the guest set their empty cup on its tray, that weight triggered the doll to turn around completely and return to the hostess, who could stop the doll's motion by lifting the empty cup off the tray to refill it. She traced the lid of the cup, grateful too that it had not been broken, crammed into that box. How could she hide it so that he would not see that she had rescued it from the attic?

She looked reluctantly back at the stairs and the open attic door. She would not put the doll back. Who knew how long it would be before he forgot the pole again. She'd have to get the ladder back in place and the door closed, or he would know what she'd done and take the pictures and doll back, and probably beat her.

She'd seen how he used the pole to force the ladder back into its retracted position, until it clicked into place, and then used the pole to close the door and re-latch it. But, she hadn't realized how much harder it was. The wooden ladder was heavy. After six failed attempts, she began to wonder if she was strong enough to do it at all.

Disaster. Now she'd be caught for sure.

She rubbed her wet eyes, and sat back on the floor, trying to memorize the pictures through her tear-blurred vision. She had one night to make the most of these gifts before they'd be taken from her.

* * * * *

She carried the doll over to the tea service area, and knelt at the charcoal burner embedded in the floor. She suspended a cast iron pot above the charcoal and wet ash, to heat the water. She pressed some matcha—powdered tea—through a sieve, and then put three heaping teaspoons into the cup. Koicha used twice the powder and half the water as the usual thin tea, usucha. She ladled hot water over the matcha, and stirred it using a bamboo tea whisk.

With the ritual complete, she took a sip of the koicha, and savored the warm thick taste of it. She set the doll facing her, in the approximate position where a guest might be sitting, and then set the cup on the tea-serving doll's tray, expecting it to carry it back to her.

But it did not.

Instead, the doll lifted the cup of koicha to its ceramic face, for all the world like it was sipping deeply from a barrel. The doll's ceramic features seemed to warm and ease, transformed to flesh, and its eyes shone like fireflies. The handsome miniature man gave her a bow. "Daughter of the many daughters I have served, how may I help?"

Hikari gasped, and choked back an astonished sob. If the doll could come alive, that meant that the world was as strange and magical as her mother had believed.

This offered her help and hope, but also a sharp stab of guilt. It was the first time she had fully allowed herself to accept that she had killed her parents with her disrespectful gesture. She closed her eyes, willing it to be a dream. Better that she was trapped now without hope, than accept that.

The doll came over and placed its tiny hand in hers. "Don't cry. The night can be cruel, but the morning is kind. Tell me what you need, and then sleep, and see what the morning brings."

She should never have disobeyed her mother. It was all her fault. She pointed sadly at the attic ladder. "Unless you can get the ladder retracted, and the door latched, it doesn't matter. He will take you and the pictures from me, and I'll be alone again."

The doll bowed to her, and then grew to the size of a man, and easily pushed the ladder back into place, and re-sealed the latch. "Done."

Hikari laughed through her tears. "Did you clean the shop for her? She never worked as hard as I have these last few months."

The doll nodded. "It was our secret." He began to clean the shop, moving so quickly that she could barely see him.

Hikari watched for several minutes, and then lay down on her mat, with the pictures tucked beneath. Her chest ached from grief and fear and the physical exertion of crying. It would feel good to sleep, even as she wondered if this was only a dream, and she would wake to an unmagical but less guilt-haunted world, and the chores that she should have been completing during her search of the attic.

* * * * *

In the morning, the chores were still done, and more perfectly than she had ever managed. The doll lay dormant beside her, and she just had time to hide him within the roll of her sleeping mat before her master returned.

Maybe it was better for the world to be as strange as her mother had believed. By the third day of Hayao's help, she was more rested than she had been in weeks, and, as a consequence, lovelier.

This proved less advantageous than she might have thought.

Her master, her father's old partner, spoke with such careless exuberance about her tireless and exacting skills as a servant, and her charm and grace as a young woman, that a passer-by became obsessed with the idea of buying her for himself.

* * * * *

The man who wanted to buy Hikari from her guardian was Mihails Ozols. He was a Russian-educated Lett, a Latvian, who had been an officer in the Russo-Japanese war. He had shared first in the humiliation of his empire at the Japanese triumph in 1904, and had shared second in the humiliation of his peers at having their manor houses burned by Latvian peasants in the uprising in 1905. His way of life and empire were dying. He fled to the Northwest with his witch of a mother, as a homesteader, determined to rebuild in a wild isolated frontier enclave, where he could be undisturbed by the headlong race to a chaotic future where Russia and nobility itself passed out of relevancy.

He'd claimed his 160 acres, and picked the densest and remotest forest that he could find, far to the north and east of the city.

He hated the Japanese for the defeat in the war. He'd not expected to find them here in Seattle where he had come to buy supplies, and it pleased him to imagine one of their daughters waiting on him hand and foot.

The two men found Hikari together to tell her the news, and gave her only a few minutes to pack her things, as Mihails was eager to return to his forest home.

* * * * *

When Hikari heard the news, she gathered up the pictures, and the doll, and as much matcha and tea-making supplies as she could fit in the small knapsack given to her by her new master.

They traveled for many days deeper and deeper into the forest. Mihails Ozols, who had instructed her to call him "Master Ozols," rode his horse, and she walked beside.

At last they reached their destination. She saw that her new master had apparently built a peculiarly isolated manor house in the middle of his forest.

"This is my home, where you will be my servant. Mine and my mother's. Do not make any noise that will draw my mother's attention before I've had a chance to explain what I've done to her. Even I fear her."

She tried to stay quiet then, stunned by how quickly her captor had become an ally to obey because she had been given something even worse to fear, but the hideous fact that her situation might be even worse than she had imagined on the long trudge through the forest bubbled up in her throat and behind her eyes, and she let out a sob, and then began to cry in earnest, choking herself with the effort to not cry, but unable to stop.

An old woman on a black horse burst from the tree line, and rode up to them. "What is this?" the old woman asked Master Ozols, looking towards Hikari.

"I have bought a servant for the house," he answered quickly.

"Ha!" she shrieked. "I do not believe you. She lacks the wit even to stop crying like a baby. You have bought a play-thing, when we needed a servant."

"Test her, then. I have her master's word she works quickly and well."

The old woman turned to Hikari. "Tomorrow, while I am out and my son is sleeping, look in the fifty old sugar bags stacked in the kitchen pantry. I have packed many dried herbs, mostly Linden flower from the old country, in those bags. Count and clean each dried leaf before I return tomorrow, and also make us a fine supper, or I will kill you, and grind your bones in my mortar to add to my tea."

The next morning, Hikari fetched water from the well, and made koicha to wake Hayao. She studied her supply of matcha nervously. She had enough for at least a week more. She considered making the koicha slightly weaker so that the supply would last longer, but she quickly rejected the idea. Her mother had told her that strong tea brought a new friend, and weak tea cost one. She couldn't risk losing Hayao.

Hikari and Hayao were able to complete the old woman's task, but only through Hayao's magic.

When the old woman returned, she ate the supper greedily, bones and all, giving Master Ozols only scraps and Hikari nothing. She appeared angry that Hikari had not failed her test, but agreed that she had done all that was asked.

"I am still not convinced," the old woman warned. "The dried herbs are ready, but in the hall closet, you will find 50 bags of caraway seeds. Each seed must be individually counted, cleaned, and crushed before I return, or I will kill you, and grind your bones in my mortar to add to my tea. And I am still expecting you to make a fine supper."

* * * * *

This time, however, the old woman found her son where Hikari could not hear, and instructed him to wake early and watch the girl through a secret hole in the kitchen wall, and learn by what means she was doing the impossible tasks so quickly. "I will learn her magic," the old woman explained, "and take it from her before I kill her." The old woman knew something of magic herself, having learned herb-lore and other tricks from her own mother in Latvia.

* * * * *

Hikari waited until the appointed time, and began to prepare a cup of koicha, unaware that Master Ozols watched and listened from behind the wall.

She talked to herself as she worked, deliberating. "Strong tea will bring the help I need. But, should I make it stronger, since we must do so much? Hayao will try to help me, regardless of whether his aid will be enough, since I am the one who makes the tea. No, I won't change my mother's recipe. It will suffice to make him strong enough and fast enough to succeed at this."

She gave the doll a cup of koicha, and Hayao awoke and responded, "Daughter of the many daughters I have served, how may I help?" as he always did. She explained the task, and showed him the tools that she had gathered. They began to work.

* * * * *

Master Ozols hurried to the stable and mounted his horse, and rode out into the forest towards a meeting place he had established with his mother.

"The girl has a doll. She makes tea for it, Japanese-style, and it wakes a demon inside that grows to the shape of a man, and helps her do the work. He moves so fast that you can barely see what he is doing."

The old woman cackled. "So now I know her secret. We shall take her doll from her, and make it work for us.

I'll take the doll, and you throw her in the oven, and we'll bake her for our supper."

Master Ozols did not like the sound of that, but said nothing. He knew better than to argue with his mother.

* * * * *

When the old woman and Master Ozols returned together, the old woman appeared again angry that Hikari had not failed her test, but agreed that she had done all that was asked.

"I am convinced," the old woman said, while eating all of the food that had been prepared for supper. "You shall be our servant, as my son wanted. Go, kneel beside my son who is your master, and has pleaded so earnestly for your life."

Hikari was surprised and relieved. She went to kneel in front of Master Ozols, and thanked him genuinely for protecting her from his mother.

But then he seized her in his arms and held her captive.

The old woman recovered the tea-serving doll from Hikari's belongings. "Foolish child. You thought to trick me with your magic, but now I have taken yours."

Hikari wept, and appealed to Master Ozols to spare her life, but he shook his head and shoved her into the oven, and locked her within. But, he did not yet heat the oven, moved by her innocent pleas, so she was simply trapped.

"Should I fetch you water from the well?" he asked his mother.

When Master Ozols returned with the water, the old woman heated the water in the kitchen samovar, and used the herbs that Hikari and the doll had ground to make a cup of tea following her own recipe. These were the strongest herbs and seeds, picked and gathered when the fields were in bloom in the old country on Midsummer's Eve, solstice night, when herbs are strongest and most potent. She added ground human bone from her private supply, from past victims.

"Now this is tea," she thought. Latvian tea. Linden flower strengthened the heart, and caraway seeds strengthened the stomach. The old woman knew that the stolen doll servant would be even stronger, faster, braver, and more powerful when he drank this. She filled a cup and placed it on the doll's tray.

The doll took a sip of the tea, and then several more draughts, and grew to human size, and then even bigger, taller and broader than a man could be, a giant. "You who are not the daughter of the many daughters I have served, why have you summoned me?"

The old woman began to rattle off the many chores that she could imagine having a strong and fast servant such as him complete.

Hayao laughed. "Did you think I would serve you because you can make a stronger and more bone-magical tea than pretty Hikari? I serve where there is strength of heart, and bonds of loyalty forged over generations. But, I thank you for the power that you have lent me." He pushed Master Ozols out of the way with the slightest of effort, tossing him off his feet and into the corner where he slumped unconscious, and then freed Hikari from the oven.

The old woman grabbed the stone pestle from the counter top and brandished it at Hayao. "Stay back!"

"You have been cruel to Hikari, and thought to enslave us both. Why should I spare you?"

The old woman hesitated, and then lowered the pestle. "Spare me and my son, and in exchange I will give you the power to have a son of your own. I know a curse that will take your power—it will make me as strong as you are now, and it will leave you as weak as I am now, but you will be human, and able to do all that a man can do."

* * * * *

Hikari and Hayao walked back to Seattle, both human, hand in hand.

* * * * *

In the years that followed, once a week, Hikari visited her parents' graves and brought them fresh flowers and stories of her life. Eventually, years later, she brought her own son and daughter as well. They could picture her parents from her treasured photographs, but went grudgingly. They found their mother old-fashioned and foolish, as all subsequent generations do.

However, Hikari, unlike her mother, thought there were some traditions and superstitions that should be followed exactly, and others that benefited from updating, as times changed. There was magic in the world, but all things thought to be magic were not. Her tea might have been weaker in some regards compared to the old woman's, but she had not lost a friend for it. Some superstitions were just that. Her children wouldn't really wet their beds if they played with fire. That was just a tale to keep children safe.

She forgave herself for any hurt she had caused her parents by disrespecting them, and let go of the question of whether she had unnaturally hastened their deaths.

The tea house, which she was eventually able to buy from her father's partner, prospered as long as Japantown prospered, but that too ended many years later as the world changed and the place of the Japanese immigrants with it.

* * * * *

And this was life, she reflected, sharing a cup of tea with Hayao, who was both her dearest friend and the father of her children, as they sat together in the cramped space of an internment camp. Though they both thought of how his magic might have helped in this dark time, neither regretted the choices they had made.

It was not necessarily happily ever after, this life, but a deep warm swallow of gain and loss, of koicha and usucha, strong and weak, thick and thin, old and new, bitter and sweet, magical and mundane. And like tea itself, most satisfying when shared.

DID YOU ENJOY THIS BOOK?

Let us know by posting a review at Amazon.com and Goodreads.com. And be sure to tell your friends on Facebook and Twitter about this and other titles from Evil Jester Press

THE QUARRY

Mark Allan Gunnells Trade Paperback $13.95 Kindle eBook $2.99

"Mark Allen Gunnells is ready to thrill fans once again with his tale of ancient evil, *The Quarry*. Once this beast of a book gets its hooks in you, it won't let go. Gunnells' voice is stronger than ever and instantly recognizable as his own—the first sign of a truly great writer. Count me in as a big fan, already looking forward to the next one!" –James Newman, author of *Midnight Rain* and *Animosity*

EVIL JESTER DIGEST VOLUME ONE

Edited by Peter Giglio Trade Paperback $9.95 Kindle eBook $2.99

10 Stunning Stories from the Masters and Rising Stars of Horror Fiction.

GPS by Rick Hautala
DUST DEVIL by Gary Brandner
SHARPE IS EXTRAORDINARY by David Dunwoody
THE GIRL WHO DROWNED by Tracy L. Carbone
DUST AT THE CENTER OF ALL THINGS by John F.D. Taff
LOOK BEHIND YOU by Eric Shapiro
LONE WOLF by Gregory L. Norris
WIDDERSHINS by Hollie Snider
A GENTLEMAN'S FOLLY by Phil Hickes
And the novelette THE END OF SUMMER by Aric Sundquist.

MOONDEATH

Rick Hautala Trade Paperback $17.95 Kindle eBook $2.99

"One of the best horror novels I've read in the last two years!"
– Stephen King (1980)

"Rick Hautala's writing shines with dedication, hard earned craft, and devotion" –Peter Straub

For the first time in more than twenty years, *New York Times* Bestselling novelist Rick Hautala's first novel is back in print! With cover art by the legendary Glenn Chadbourne and an all new introduction from bestselling author Christopher Golden, the Evil Jester Press edition of *Moondeath* is a must have for every horror fan.

The Fierce and Unforgiving Muse

Gregory L. Norris Trade Paperback $19.95 Kindle eBook $3.99

Twenty-six tales from the terrifying mind of Gregory L. Norris.

"In my experience of seven years on *Voyager*, I do not believe I have encountered a writer for whom I have greater respect in terms of intelligence, understanding, and talent. There is no one more capable to pen such a volume as *Muse* and, also, to do it so beautifully." –Kate Mulgrew, *Star Trek: Voyager*

HELP! WANTED: Tales of On-the-Job Terror

Edited by Peter Giglio Trade Paperback $14.95 Kindle eBook $2.99

"*Help! Wanted* is a rollicking, creepy, crazy, and thoroughly unnerving collection of work-related horror stories by the cream of today's horror crop. Each story is as stingingly fresh as a razor cut!" –Jonathan Maberry, *New York Times* Bestselling author of *Dust & Decay* and *Patient Zero*

Features stories by Stephen Volk, Jeff Strand, Joe McKinney, Gary Brandner, Lisa Morton, Vince A. Liaguno, Mark Allan Gunnells, David Dunwoody, Amy Wallace, Scott Bradley, Eric Shapiro, Gregory L. Norris, and many more!

Cameron's Closet

Gary Brandner Trade Paperback $13.95 Kindle eBook $2.99

Brandner's classic horror novel returns to print! Features an all new introduction from Joe McKinney.

Balance (a zombie novella)

Peter Giglio Trade Paperback $9.95

"Balance is a grim and melancholy zombie story. Peter Giglio brings his A-game to this disturbing tale." –Jonathan Maberry, *New York Times* Bestselling author of *Dead of Night* and *Dust & Decay*

"A harrowing new perspective on the apocalypse. Giglio goes for the heart as well as the jugular." –David Dunwoody, author of *Empire's End* and *Unbound & Other Tales*

THE BLAST
A worldwide snowstorm that brings with it a terminal virus.

THE DEAD
Rise!
But something deep within hasn't died. The thing they loved most when alive still burns bright, at odds with a predacious hunger they can't control or understand.

GEOFF & AMANDA Have survived The Blast. The bad news: 650 miles of treacherous, zombie infested road separates them.

And time is running out for Amanda!

Short of a Picnic

Eric Shapiro Trade Paperback $9.95 Kindle eBook $2.99

A brilliant collection by the acclaimed author of *The Devoted* and *Stories for the End of the World*. Twelve stories. Twelve troubled minds.

Printed in Great Britain
by Amazon